MASQUE WORLD

"is the third story in the Anthony Villiers series that also includes STAR WELL and THE THURB REVOLUTION. . . . It makes for a charming creation. . . . Panshin . . . can introduce both a robot butler and a lecherous old procurator, the latter given to dropping overripe melons down palace stairwells at other men's wives. And he can introduce an imperial envoy into a real identity crisis *via* a Trog suit. . . .

"Read the book. Stop asking silly questions."

—Algis Budrys, *Galaxy*

MASQUE WORLD

"is not just better than the competition; it is, by any standards, a very funny book, and a joy to read."

—*Fantasy and Science Fiction*

MASQUE WORLD

"may by out by the time you see this. Get it."

—*Analog*

Ace Science Fiction
by
ALEXEI PANSHIN

The ANTHONY VILLIERS Adventures

STAR WELL
THE THURB REVOLUTION
MASQUE WORLD

RITE OF PASSAGE

with Cory Panshin:

EARTH MAGIC

ALEXEI PANSHIN

ace books

A Division of Charter Communications Inc.
A GROSSET & DUNLAP COMPANY
360 Park Avenue South
New York, New York 10010

MASQUE WORLD

Copyright © 1969 by Alexei Panshin

An ACE Book

Cover art by Vincent Di Fate

This Ace printing: November 1978

Printed in U.S.A.

for Lee Hoffman
and Chip Delany

Early in 1463 of the Common Era. On Delbalso, a semi-autonomic dependency of the Nashuite Empire.

1

CASTLE ROCK rises above the town, out of the town, a massive block, a monolith. There is a steep slope behind the last gabled peak of buildings, possible to climb when green, less likely in white. And then the face of the block—black by night, and then a marbled gray-white, white and then orange, orange and then black—but always impossible. There is a door at the foot of Castle Rock and a road that leads down into the town.

To the handful of Empire administrators, petty officials and janitors who live within Castle Rock, it is "The Castle." They take that seriously, and by a metaphorical transposition of their physical situation, they imagine themselves looming large in local lives, which, of course, they don't. Since in the main they do not venture outside, they are seldom disabused.

To the people of the town, Castle Rock is "The Rock." The janitors are an unknown quantity, since they do so seldom venture out of their fastness. The rock itself is a physical presence, a common fact, a landmark to be kept on the left when going out, and the right returning. It can hardly be ignored, but it is only a rock, and, as you can imagine, the people of the town have difficulty mustering inordinate respect for an object held in such easy contempt by birds.

The charterboat landed on Castle Rock when the red sun was at the cold world's edge and the Rock was orange, its best and brightest face, its brave smile bravely held in the face of coming dark. Two passengers with small luggage debarked. The wind whipped at them and then they went within the Rock.

Every human being who has ever lived has extended the range of the species. There isn't one among us who hasn't thought, said or done something unique. New ideas, new recipes, new fashions. New tunes, new games, new places for people to play.

Since Jerzy McBe was human, he, too, had extended the range of the species, but not by much. He had his limitations.

He was one of the janitors of Empire, thin, brown, and at the end of unused youth. His job was uninteresting and he performed it inadequately. He inspected the papers of travelers to Delbalso and he inspected the papers of those departing. He had done the work for two years and not only had he not earned a promotion to more agreeable labor, he now knew less about his business than the day he started.

He finished checking through the family party leaving on the charterboat. Man, one; wives, two; children, four—and the crated remnants of several generations of

2

summering on Delbalso. McBe had checked this same family on at least three previous occasions, but they were not among the very few in the world whom McBe recognized at sight. Their name was in his hand, where he knew where to find it, not in his mind, which was a less ordered place. The name was Gramineous.

The family had rather more baggage this time, as had the majority of those leaving Delbalso these days. To McBe it just seemed like a lot of baggage. The passage of the Winter-Summer Laws had escaped his attention. He slept with a night light and he had never set foot outside the Castle.

"Have a good trip," he said, handing the man's name back. To inbound travelers, he said, "Have a nice stay." But he still hadn't been outside the Castle.

McBe checked the time. He had a schedule, and the closer he came to keeping it, the safer he felt.

There were two passengers from the charterboat. One was a young man, well-born, well-dressed, but unprepossessing. Behind him was a large alien, brown, furry and friendly in appearance. McBe didn't trust appearances, and he didn't like aliens. His immediate superior was an alien of a different kind and his attentions had always made McBe nervous.

"Papers," said McBe.

The young man reached a slight hand within his coat. He was small and lean and his nose and cheekbones were prominent. His long brown hair was caught and tied, the prisoner of a light green ribbon. He wore a serviceable cloak and simple clean ruffles.

"My papers, sir," he said, presenting the narrow maroon booklet.

McBe didn't like his manner, so he took the papers

3

and leaned back. He thumbed them instead of stamping them. He *hmm*ed.

He said, "In your picture you lack a mustache, Mr. Villiers."

Villiers said, "That is correct. The picture is some six years old. I grew my mustache during a recent vacation."

"You should have had your papers emended," McBe said.

The alien said, "Is easy enough to change."

He had eyes of bulgy blue and a fuzzy white belly, and McBe could not recall having seen his like before. He loomed over Villiers' shoulder, seized pen from McBe's pocket and book from hand, made a peculiar throbbing noise that McBe found unsettling, and drew a careful mustache of proper dimension on the picture.

"There," he said. "Is mended."

Villiers picked it up and studied it while McBe continued to stare. Villiers touched his mustache for comparison. He was young enough that six years had changed him substantially, but the alien's adscription did much to harmonize man and likeness.

"You're right," he said, nodding. "I do believe you've caught my very spirit."

He held the picture for McBe's inspection. "Don't you agree that the addition of a mustache gives me a gravity that formerly I lacked? I don't know why I didn't grow one years ago when my need was greater."

McBe was confirmed in his dislike of the man.

The alien made the throbbing noise again: "*Thurb.*" He had the contented look of a toad in summer.

Villiers said, "Perhaps I should grow a beard as well." He considered the picture again, and then looked about for the pen. "Do you mind?"

4

MASQUE WORLD

His intention caused McBe to snatch the pen up.
"No!" he said, which Villiers rightly took to mean that
he did mind.

McBe said to the alien, "It is a serious matter to
deface official papers."

McBe said to Villiers, "A very serious matter. There
are penalties. It is a very good thing for you that you
didŋ't compound the offense."

McBe said to the alien, "Do you realize . . ."

McBe said to Villiers, "Your papers, if you
please." He thumbed to the front. He moved his finger
as he read.

McBe said to the alien, "Do you realize that you
might be fined a full five royals, and subjected to
penalties under four statutes?" He held up the book and
pointed to the statute numbers.

McBe said to Villiers, whom he didn't like, "And
you should know better, sir."

"Your pardon," said Villiers. "I'm sure he intended no harm. If the picture needs replacement, as
you suggest, then no harm has been done. Let us
replace the picture, and all will be as it should."

McBe leaned back and looked at him through narrowed eyes. The effect—for McBe was not totally
without presence—was redolent of authority.

"Are you trying to teach me my business?" he
asked, the age-old question of authority challenged.
"Defacement is defacement. It may be enough to
change the picture, and it may not. I think I shall have to
have a closer look at your papers in any case."

If Villiers had deferred properly, McBe would have
been ready to let him go his own way, but instead the
young man looked down his cool nose and said, "Really? A matter of routine, I suppose?"

"Yes," said McBe. "A matter of routine. I'm sure you understand."

He checked the time, and the thought of cost to his schedule made him more peevish. If his schedule suffered appreciably, he expected to show Mr. Villiers a thing or two about bureaucracy.

He pointed to the alien. "Next, there. Let me see your papers. Pa-pers."

"To be sure," the alien said, and presented his book.

McBe flipped through it. "Well," he said. "At least you haven't marked your own book."

He stamped it, *bam*, and handed it back. "Listen—it was very wrong of you to mark the book. Never do anything like that again. Now follow the yellow line and it will take you out."

Don't think it strange that McBe challenged Villiers rather than the alien. McBe knew to a fine degree exactly what he was capable of coping with.

The alien looked at him and the black pits in his blue blue eyes pulsed questioningly. For a panicked moment, McBe thought he might make that noise again.

He drew breath and said, "Shoo. Go along. I'm done with you."

The alien said, "I am done with you, too. Is agreed. Goodbye."

Villiers said, "Goodbye."

McBe said nothing. He sat unmoving until the alien had padded off to find where the yellow line had it in mind to go. Then he swished his nasal passages, rose and said, "Come along."

But he left Villiers' papers on the desk. Villiers rescued them and handed them over when McBe suddenly turned halfway to the exit. Villiers raised his eyebrows. He had parallel wrinkles over each brow that rose into prominence as the brows rose, and seconded every comment they made.

It was excellent natural equipment and Villiers made good use of it. McBe was sure then that he disliked Villiers. It took little to confirm a suspicion like that. He nodded coldly for Villiers to proceed.

Slyne was an Orthodoxou. Orthodoxous are unmistakable, clothed by nature in black velvet, bodies bulbous, heads enclosed but for the wet tip of the nose in the metal lattice of their sensory amplifiers. Slyne was an unmistakable Orthodoxou, the only one in the entire Imperial Service. He was the first. He had the feeling of being watched, justified to some extent by his promotion to his present position on Delbalso after his success in a bit of amateur detection that keyed in significantly to the Diced Strawberry Affair on Able II. (That was a code name—the reality was more sinister.) His ambition was to be an Inspector General some day, an example for the Empire and for other Orthodoxous of what an Orthodoxou might be.

Orthodoxous have no talent for the construction of elaborate artificial systems, but they admire rigmarole immensely and find great satisfaction in making the most of it. Naturally, Imperial Service would have great appeal for them, so if Slyne had the feeling of being watched, it might have been because other distant eyes were peering brightly, observing his good works.

Slyne was earnest and diligent, and unable to understand why he was not loved. He was not loved because he was not lovable.

He was McBe's superior, looking for McBe, as he so

often was. He liked McBe too well for McBe's comfort. He was always asking what McBe was doing. He was always hanging about trying to entertain McBe with a recital of Empire regulations, or some boring story of a minor exploit that had boosted him into his present position of niggling authority.

Slyne found McBe in his "office"—his cubicle. He had a young man with him. Slyne sniffed at them, his wet nose wriggling through the grillwork.

McBe shied, and then said defensively, "I have defaced and outdated papers here. I was going to run a Random Depth Inspection on them."

The young man said nothing. Slyne wriggled his nose.

Then Slyne said, "Well, continue, then."

McBe looked at the time. "I'm behind schedule," he said. He shoved the papers at Slyne. "Here. Why don't you take over? Could you, please?"

He plunged out of the room and then kitty-corner into the sanctuary of the toilet. It was on his schedule for the end of the day, but he was more abrupt about it than he usually was. The door slid shut behind him and locked and a discreet green light went on above.

The Orthodoxou looked at the young man. More properly, he looked in the direction of the young man. It was hard to tell exactly what he was looking at behind the amplifier.

"You defaced your papers?" he said.

"No," said the young man.

"How are the papers defaced?"

"A mustache," said the young man. He showed the picture.

Slyne took the papers and peered at them, then at their bearer. "A mustache? Ornamental lip hair?"

"True. I wear a mustache."

"I see that you do."

"My picture showed no mustache."

"It should have. It is best to keep these things regular, Mr. Villiers."

"So Mr. McBe said."

"Is that when you defaced your papers?" Slyne eyed the door to the toilet, but the green light was still on. He turned back to Villiers. "It's against regulations to deface official papers, you know." He named the regulations. He knew his regulations.

"I'm sure that it is," said Villiers, "and quite properly, too. But as it happens, it was not I who defaced the picture, but another passenger, apparently with insufficient grasp of the basic importance of official papers. We traveled here in the same ship. A most remarkable character, and not predictable."

"You claim that it was another that defaced the papers?"

"Yes."

"Where is this other passenger?"

"Gone. Mr. McBe stamped his papers and sent him on his way."

"That seems unusual," said Slyne. "McBe should have kept him in hand until the matter has had its due. I think we had best ask McBe for an explanation. McBe!"

And there you have the value of a sensory amplifier. The toilet door had just opened and McBe had emerged. Slyne spoke without turning. It was almost a good enough trick for a party.

McBe came slowly to the door. "Yes, sir."

Slyne said, "How was the picture defaced?"

Villiers looked on with calm interest. His manner

throughout was unconcerned. Whether it was innocent interest or arrogant assurance that he displayed was a matter for question. It might have been either.

McBe said, "The alien marked it."

"The alien?"

"There was an alien in my line, just off the charterboat. He marked the picture. But the papers are still outdated."

"You let him go?"

"His papers looked all right."

"What kind of alien was it?"

McBe said, "I don't know. Excuse me, sir. I'm supposed to be off duty now."

He really did have a schedule. He needed one, since the Imperial Service did not see fit to direct his life with the fineness that he required. His schedule held his life together.

Slyne said, "Mr. McBe, you will not be done until I tell you that you are done."

"I *warned* the alien," McBe said defensively.

"That's very commendable. Describe the alien, please."

"Well, furry. Bigger than you. Big blue eyes."

"A Trog," said Villiers quietly.

"A Trog!" exclaimed Slyne.

And well he might exclaim. Trogs are Restricted, confined since the end of the War of Orion's Ear to their two home solar systems. Trogs are strange and uncertain creatures and only some fifty are allowed to travel with even relative ease. You would be fortunate to see one in a lifetime.

"Did you examine his Permit to Travel? Did you check his Red Card?"

"No," said McBe. "I guess I didn't."

Slyne looked at him reproachfully. He wasn't quite sure why he allowed McBe to continue in service, except that he liked the way McBe smelled. It is an article of faith with some Orthodoxous that each of them shall search for that elusive and ultimate odor that once found rules life. Slyne had always thought this romantic foolishness, but that was before he had come to Delbalso and met McBe. He was less smugly certain now that the tradition was without foundation. He felt giddy around McBe, and was ashamed because he knew it bad for his ambition.

McBe said, "He must have been too clever for me."

"That would explain things," said Slyne. "What color was the Trog?"

It is a fact that Trogs, unlike humans, are significantly color-coded. Peasants are a basic gray metamorphosing to olive. Soldiers are white striped with black. And scholars are always brown, solid brown, nothing but brown, never anything but brown, and that is that. If you were a Trog and you weren't brown, you wouldn't even be *interested*.

McBe thought about the color of the beast. Since he thought in black and white, it was difficult for him to remember things like that. "Brown," he said at last.

That was true, but insufficient. Villiers knew better: the Trog had had a white belly and faint black stripes on his back. But Villiers did not correct McBe, perhaps out of politeness.

"A scholar," concluded Slyne, demonstrating the deleterious effects of imperfect data on conclusion. "Perhaps we should begin to look for him in libraries and educational institutions."

"We?" said McBe.

"Of course, we," said Slyne, wriggling his nose through the wire cage. "This is a Restricted Sentient. The Empire doesn't set restrictions idly. We'll have to find him, and start now."

McBe looked at the time and whimpered. Slyne looked at Villiers, who withdrew his attention. Slyne drew McBe aside. This involved a paw placed against McBe's chest, a bird cage next to his ear, and the sound of an occasional whuffle of deeply-breathed air. McBe hardly flinched. Give him credit.

Slyne said quietly, "A new Administrator is due to assume authority here at any moment. Think of your job, McBe."

"A new Administrator?" said McBe. It had been the main topic of conversation within the Rock for a month but McBe hadn't been listening. That is, he knew, he had heard, but the information had not penetrated his defenses.

"Yes," said Slyne. His wet nose touched McBe's earlobe and he whuffled. McBe's shoulder shuddered slightly, but you couldn't call that a flinch.

"If this Trog is a scholar, it may not be so dangerous, but, even so, it must be found. It is up to you and me. I don't think that you have been doing your job as your job should be done. McBe, I shall be watching you. You shall show me a new McBe. And together we will find this Trog. If it has a proper set of papers, it may go its way. If it does not, you and I shall take it into custody. If you perform well, you will be excused. But if you do not perform well—or if trouble should come of this—I shall sacrifice you to the new Administrator. I have my career to bear in mind. If you care to continue to wear Empire livery, it had best be a new McBe. Starting this minute. Now straighten up.''

This sounded impressively threatening, and in fact McBe did feel threatened. Though he did his work badly, and took no pleasure in it, the thought of searching for a different employ in which greater demands might be made of him was genuinely frightening.

Slyne snuffled and his nose nuzzled McBe's ear. McBe had more latitude than he knew. But since he had no appreciation of the fact, he straightened up and tried to look as though he cared about the alien, as though he cared about doing a proper job, as though he didn't mind abandoning his imperative need to put on his night light and crawl under the covers. Outside? At night? He almost broke, but he was too frightened, so he bent.

"Yes, sir," he said. It was just as well that he had already observed the previous part of his agenda.

Slyne turned and said, "And now, Mr. Villiers. We must talk about your defective papers."

McBe made a quick swipe of ear against shoulder, and then became aware that Villiers had observed him, which caused a rush of cold followed by radiant resentment.

Villiers turned his attention to Slyne. He said, "Perhaps the matter can be settled with some ease."

He reached within his coat and produced a large flat wallet, which he opened.

McBe said, "Bribery?" He didn't say it too loudly. He got halfway into the word, and then finished it as a question.

Villiers said, "Sir, while it might be possible to bribe you, nothing in our short acquaintance leads me to the belief that there could be any conceivable benefit in doing so. Accordingly, I shall forego the opportunity you have just proffered. I trust you will not take it amiss, and will forgive me if I have misjudged you."

To Slyne, he said, "I thought to supplement my papers with various items of identification. If you find them satisfactory, perhaps you will allow me to travel on the planet and may monish my papers as you please in the meantime. Here, to begin, is my Patent."

"You have a title?" Slyne asked, to and by appearances impressed.

"Viscount Charteris," said Villiers. He said it with the straightest of faces.

First, out of the Rock came the Trog, following the yellow line.

Brown, basically. Friendly in appearance.

The sun had set by then, and the Rock was black with night. The air was cool. The Trog tested the evening and then followed the will of the road down into the town.

After some search, he found Joralemon House of the Delbalso Monist Association. The Monist Association had a house in each of the quarters of Delbalso. Joralemon House was a rambling pile, its palisade enclosing armfuls of gardens and buildings. It had once been smaller, but after the way of Monist Associations, it was still growing. Joralemon House had fourteen gates and doors.

The Trog padded around the perimeter. He paused at one gate and then passed on. Eventually he stopped outside a door and in the fullness of time the door opened.

"Hello," he said to the Warder. "I am Torve. I wish to see Badrian Beaufils."

"What is your business?" asked the Warder.

"We are pen pals," said Torve the Trog.

"Oh, well, come in, then," said the man, and welcomed him within. "Now that I think of it, I believe I've heard him make mention of you."

He closed the great wooden door behind them.

Second, out of the Rock came Villiers. He was out of difficulty and into the cool clear air five minutes after he announced himself. It is clear—a title can be an advantage. Imagine the coils if he had not declared the game over by revealing himself.

In fact, however, it hardly seems proper behavior. It is certainly fair for a noble to go incognito, just as it is for a common man to occasionally assume a weekend title. But if nobles are going to go incognito, they should have the grace to stay incognito come the last muffin on the plate. But they never do. No, they stand, announce themselves, and in the stunned silence they gobble the muffin. Clearly they are taught the wrong things in childhood.

Villiers failed to look properly ashamed of himself. He threw his cloak back and looked around for directions to a city car. He was smiling. And then he laughed out of sheer exuberant good spirits.

Taught all the wrong things in childhood.

Last, out of the Castle came Slyne and McBe. Slyne had buttressed memory with research and now knew Trogs for exactly the uncertain creatures they were. Empire Regulations were the guide.

Empire Regulations are quite specific. Trogs are not to be allowed to travel. Their principles of behavior not yielding to ready analysis, they must be considered dangerous. Even scholars. If you like, especially scholars.

The doors opened at the foot of the Rock. They stood for a moment looking out at the Night. There was light from the spray of stars and a glow from the town, but mainly it was dark. McBe felt dismay.

"Come along," said Slyne. He bent and began to cast back and forth. And then he set out, following his amplified senses down the hill.

McBe took a deep breath, and followed after Slyne. The pain in his stomach was only sharp for a time, and then it grew numb. He held his breath as long as he could, and when at last he had to, let it go.

To his real surprise, he did not die.

2

IN THESE DAYS when any man can comfortably dance naked in a snowstorm (Imagine careening down a long and leaning hillside, knee-high in snow, free flakes swirling about you shank to thatch. You kick and scatter the snow, start slides, throw it over your shoulders in scattering double handfuls, hop and caper in the gray and white twilight.) it remains true that the general run of mankind is sufficiently attached to their clothing to forego the opportunity. Theirs be the loss—I am assured by those who know that it is an uncommonly rewarding experience.

Some—simple folk, mostly—plead the need for pockets. If they must carry their trinkets and knickknacks about, even in the midst of an uncommonly rewarding experience, one would think they could wear a pack, or carry a poke, or hang a little bag

17

around their neck. But they say it's not the same, and pass snowstorms by.

For many, clothing is style. Clothing is taste. Clothing is breeding, intelligence, pursuit, ambition. *Place*. Clothing defines, letting us know who and what a person is. But one naked man in a snowstorm is much like another, and these people are incapable of baring their anonymity.

And for others, clothing is identity. Without their single well-worn suit, they would have no idea of who they were. Naked in a snowstorm, they know they would be invisible and become lost. There are many people like this, most of them very much in need of an uncommonly rewarding experience, but limited and fettered by their clothing.

Even more limited and fettered by the fact that they have stuck staunchly by the very first suit of clothes they ever tried on. If you are going to be what you wear, you should try more than one style before you settle.

As an experiment, try on something strange and wild. What sweet whirling thoughts unsettle the mind? Think about them. Now, who are you?

The house was familiar to Villiers though he had never been on Delbalso before. The extended family of Mr. Jules Parini was much given to travel, and wherever they owned houses, which was widely, the houses were cut to this single pattern. They felt it lent a happy continuous thread to their otherwise discontinuous lives.

The house was in a state of disarray. Parini was being forced to leave both it and Delbalso by the Winter-Summer Laws. He had not left thus far because he lacked the money. Don't think for a minute that he was a bad provider. However, a tuition payment of no less than thirty-five royals—a figure of which Parini was secretly proud—to Miss McBurney's Justly Famous Seminary and Finishing School on Nashua on behalf of his elder daughter Louisa had left him with minimal resources.

"I didn't expect to see you," he said. "I left word."

"I received it," said Villiers. "As it happened, I had other cause to visit Delbalso. I stopped on the chance that you had not left. I count myself fortunate to find you still here."

Jules Parini wore the clothes of a rug salesman. They were far from the first suit he had tried on, but he looked in character as a rug salesman, and it suited him to look in character. Anything else might require subtlety and subtlety was not his. Louisa was at Miss McBurney's to learn subtlety.

For the most part, he was a rug salesman, ornamental. His real profession was ornamental, too. He was a con man.

The techniques of con men vary. Parini depended on brute force. He was so domineering, so inevitable, so sure, that most of the people he did business with simply let him have his way to be shut of him. He sold rugs in exactly the same way.

"I'm a pragmaticist," he would say, meaning that he had no education and he was selective about his principles.

"Let's step out on the patio," he said. Parini houses always had patios. What they grew in them varied from one planet to the next, but they had a lettuce bed and a patch of fennel when they could.

Parini looked about him, and spied his younger daughter. She was four and her name was Anne. Wondrous is the way of an eagle in the air, and a serpent upon the rock, but even more wondrous is the way of a four-year-old with a room of boxes full and empty. She made a caret, feet on the floor and head in a box. She was wearing rompers. She fished with her right hand and in her left she held a cloth doll by the foot and swung it for balance.

Parini put an arm about her middle and lifted her out of the box and set her on her feet. She immediately took a second grip farther down the doll's leg with her right hand.

Parini pointed to his vid service. Calling around, knowing what was going on, being in touch—these were the heart of his business. "Keep an eye on the service while we are on the patio," Parini said.

She said, very definitely, "I'm s'posed to be going to bed."

"Never you mind that," her father said sharply. "Just watch the service."

She said, "But Mommy will be mad at me."

"I don't care. Do as I tell you."

She trembled on the edge of tears, and then didn't cry, but did continue to tremble.

Parini led Villiers to the patio, the darkling sky open above them. "You have to be firm with children," he said. "If you want them to do as you say, you have to make them mind from the beginning. . . . I can't put my finger on it, but something about you is different."

There was a major difference. Villiers was nearly five years older. Villiers put his finger on the difference.

"Yes," he said. "I like to think I make a different order of mistake these days."

In their previous dealings, Villiers had come away poorer in pocket, not unreasonable when you realize that Parini had a living to make. Business, after all, is business, and to Parini life was business.

"Your errors were errors of youth," said Parini, without irony. Irony was another thing Louisa was supposed to learn from Miss McBurney. "In any case, shall I say it's good to see you again, Villiers? I'm not sure I approve of your methods or your companions, but nonetheless, you did see to my daughter's safety. I owe you a favor for that."

Villiers ceased to stroke his mustache. At times he would tug it on the left, but he kept the trim in balance by occasionally chewing it on the right. "Well, I'm all the more pleased to have found you, then. Do you have the papers for the Trog?"

"Why do you travel with such a chancy creature, Villiers? I'm not sure I'm doing the right thing. If this Trog deserved to travel, I'm sure the Empire would have issued it with proper papers."

"That's a considerable argument coming from your lips," said Villiers. "While I will admit that I don't understanding the Trog, he makes a very comfortable traveling companion. Have you the papers yet?"

Light flashed through the garden with the opening of a door. It was Anne in her blue rompers, still clutching the leg of the cloth doll in both hands.

"*Atensi, par,*" she said. "*Vow tendi a vizeer.*"

"Ah, Annie. Come here!"

The little girl approached slowly.

"Now present yourself. Villiers, this is my daughter Anne. Annie, this is Mr. Villiers."

"Oh!" she said, but her father made nothing of it.

She made a very good dip for a four-year-old, particularly one whose father has to dress like a rug salesman to feel really comfortable. Villiers returned the honor.

"A good learner, wouldn't you say? I have no doubt that when the time comes I can pass her into Miss McBurney's after Louisa. Now, Annie, take Mr. Villiers inside. I'll be a few minutes, Villiers." He put his hands together. "Calling around," he said, locking them, backing away. He opened his hands again, turned and disappeared inside the house.

"Boro Dad!" Annie said pensively. She didn't know what it meant exactly. It was an expression she had picked up from the neighbors.

Annie said, "Are you really Mt. Villiers?"

It had been five years and he was disguised behind a heavy brown mustache, but Miriam Parini recognized Anthony Villiers as soon as her daughter led him into the room. His walk and bearing were still the same.

Annie said, "He says he's Mr. Villiers."

"Tony!" she said. "How long have you been in the house?"

She was a pleasant woman with exophthalmic eyes that rescued her from simple plainness. She was devoted to her husband's interests. The formal charge is Aiding and Abetting.

"Not long," he said. "We passed before but you were busy and didn't see us. I certainly wouldn't have left without saying hello."

"I should hope not!" she said.

She was standing in an obstacle course of boxes. She had been making decisions. Even at the best of times, housekeeping skills were not her strongest suit, and she tended to let work accumulate until it became visible, or even necessary. Now it was acutely necessary and she was busy.

Annie said, "Is he the one?"

"Yes," said Mrs. Parini.

"Oh!" said Annie.

"Oh, Annie, you should be in bed," said her mother. "Didn't I tell you to go to bed!"

Villiers said, "I could put Annie to bed, if that would help."

"Oh, it would," said her mother.

"Annie, would you like to hear a bedtime story?"

"Oh, that's good," said Mrs. Parini. "That will give me time to straighten a bit, and then we can talk."

Annie considered the matter. It was possible, after all, that Villiers was an inexpert storyteller, in which case she could be letting herself in for all sorts of tedium.

"I guess," she said.

"She's all ready to be tucked in," her mother said.

When she was tucked, which took yet a few minutes, four-year-olds being what they are and this one having her own thoughts on her mind and her own slow way of exposing them, and when she was settled and shushed, which took one or two minutes more, Villiers told her a story. The story was called "The Hobyahs."

"Once," he said, "there was an old man and a woman and a little girl, and they all lived in a house made of hempstalks. Now the old man had a little dog named Turpie; and one night the Hobyahs came and said, 'Hobyah! Hobyah! Hobyah! Tear down the hempstalks, eat up the old man and woman, and carry off the little girl!' But little dog Turpie barked so that the Hobyahs ran off.''

That was the beginning. The ending was, ''The next night the Hobyahs took down the bag and knocked on the top of it, and said, 'Look me! Look me!' and when they opened the bag—the big dog jumped out and ate them all up: so there are no Hobyahs now.''

It was a good story, showing blatant favoritism for little girls above all the other creatures of the earth. Villiers told it well, with considerable animation and a variety of voices. He was very good at ''Look me! Look me!''

However, at the conclusion of the story, instead of applauding Villiers or telling him that it was a good story, which indeed she had thought it was, Annie said, ''I saw a dog once.''

And she said, ''I think they were *mean* to little dog Turpie.''

But she still had her own thoughts on her mind, and so she said, ''When you marry my sister, can I carry flowers?''

''Of course,'' said Villiers, ever the gentleman.

She said, ''Can I come live with you?''

It is perfectly reasonable that with a father who dressed like a rug salesman, and moreover yelled, she might wish to leave home, but Villiers was finding his sudden promotion to brother-in-law premature at the least.

Gently he said, ''Why do you think that your sister and I will marry?''

''Well, she says she's going to marry you.''

''Oh,'' said Villiers. Then, ''Did she say when?''

"No."

"Annie, do you know where Louisa is right now?"

"Uh, she's away at school."

"Yes," said Villiers. "She's at school to learn. The schools are full of books, Annie, and in those books are everything that people have learned through all the thousands of years of history. In those books it says things that your sister doesn't know, things like: 'A man who is vulgar or fallen from social position and much given to travel does not deserve a wife; and the same is true of the man who having a wife and children spends all his time at sports and rarely comes home to his family.' "

"Do you have a wife and children?"

"No," said Villiers. "But I do spend too much time in sport and travel. Once your sister has done her reading, you can be sure that she won't have any part of me."

"But those are *old* books," said Annie. She hadn't been around for long, but she had been around long enough to know what whatever things may have been like once, in these days they were very different.

"I like to travel," she said, "I like to play."

Villiers shook his head solemnly. "You should be aware then that you compromise your chances of making a successful marriage."

Hopefully, she said, "I don't think Louisa reads much."

She was finally convinced to settle for a firm promise about the flowers, and a conditional promise on living arrangements.

"I was in such terror when I heard that Louisa had been involved with a Trog," said Mrs. Parini. "But I was relieved as soon as Pavel said that you were there. I knew you wouldn't allow harm to come to Louisa."

"It would have been poor payment for your hospitality," said Villiers.

"But who knows what a Trog will do?"

"It is certain that I don't," said Villiers, "but still we must judge by result, and Louisa did come to no harm. By the way, are you aware of her designs?"

"Oh, yes," she said, "but don't speak loudly. Jules doesn't know."

"He wouldn't like the idea?"

"Well, no," she said. "I'm not sure he'd approve. After all, he has his plans. It wouldn't do for Louisa to marry just anyone, even you, Tony. But I think she'll get over it before long. Does she know of your mustache yet?"

"We exchange only random letters and I haven't mentioned it," said Villiers. "She's unlikely to know unless she has it from a third source."

"She never liked mustaches," said Mrs. Parini.

"Perhaps I should reconsider mine, then," said Villiers.

"Don't," said Mrs. Parini. "I think your mustache is very becoming."

Parini returned by way of the patio, bringing with him a trace of cooler air and the sound of a slow and deeply tolling bell. Villiers cocked his head at the sound.

Parini said, "We have unusual neighbors. The bell belongs to a Christian. It is one of a set he rings at peculiar hours and seasons. There's a Monist House just down the street. There used to be gypsies in the neighborhood, but they anticipated the Winter-Summer Laws and left Delbalso months ago."

His mood was notably improved, which shows what a session of calling around can do for a man who thrives upon it.

"And just as well," said Mrs. Parini. "They were a bad influence on Annie. She picked up some unfortunate phrases from them."

Parini was smiling broadly and clearly feeling good. "I have some particular news for you, Villiers. Your little affair on Star Well gave me some leverage on Nicholas Zvegintzov. His sources on Livermore may be able to produce the name you've been seeking these past months."

"Who are his sources?"

"The Red-Headed Bunny and the Black Buck."

"Well, then I am impressed. I attempted to hire their resources without success. What do you feel the information will be worth?"

"What did you offer for the information?"

"Twenty royals."

"Well, that will be a figure to talk from," Parini said.

"Fine," said Villiers. "Shall we talk about the papers again?"

"Oh," said Parini, "I'm sorry to say but they have not yet arrived. I was saying to Miriam last morning that I held greater expectations of seeing the papers than of seeing you. Did I not, Miriam?"

"Oh, yes," she said.

He continued, "Jack the Hand sent them on their way direct. He swears they will stand any scrutiny. There's a mail yet to arrive from Duden tonight. I have no doubt it will be here then. There's a scheduled delivery around peelgrunt."

"In that case, let me go and return again," Villiers

said. "I have other business here on Delbalso. I'll return after peelgrunt."

When Villiers had gone, shown to the door and into the night, Mrs. Parini said behind the closing door, "He's really quite nice."

"Villiers?"

"And you always make money from him."

"Twice."

"I don't know why you don't like him better."

"Who said I didn't like him?" said Parini. "He just isn't our sort of people. You can't really say so, can you? Now that he's grown past the stage where he will believe everything you tell him, the best policy is to keep things friendly, but distant. Businesslike."

"Well, I suppose," Mrs. Parini said.

"Of course I'm right."

"Yes, of course," she said.

"I have news," he said. "There was good word. It's definite that Treleaven is not leaving Delbalso. The flam is still codger. We'll strip him bare and be gone before morning!"

"Oh, that's wonderful," she said.

Night had firm possession of the quiet tree-lined streets as Villiers set out for the closest flitter central. There was a faint underlying chill in the air. There were no pedestrians in the street, and Villiers only saw a single City Car slide by on its overhead rail. People were locking themselves into their houses and tucking up, even though the night was not far advanced.

If thoughts of the names of assassins and, perhaps, of papers were on his mind, it would be understandable. His thoughts marched to the threnody of the

Christian's bells, swinging clear and cold over the streets stacked along the hill.

After some minutes, Villiers came in sight of the flitter post. It lay at the foot of the street slope, a rainbow pillar topped by a mushroom roof. There was a flitter waiting.

Villiers turned into the street, but before he had taken more than a few steps, he was surrounded by a group of men in identical blue.

The men—there were three—were all of sober years. Their suits were cut to no pattern that Villiers had ever seen on the street before. They consisted of knee-length pants, shirts of bright blue, and belted blue vests. And the men wore lively peaked caps, blue and nappy.

One of them said, "Are you a Marvel or Wonder?"

One must attribute their strange behavior to their unusual costumes. Men of that age are commonly a settled lot, not given to ask philosophical questions of strangers in the street chance-met. But even settled men can find a jaunty cap and feather unsettling. What questions they might be given to ask if they dressed like Socrates must be left to the imagination.

3

THERE ARE THOSE who honestly believe in the superiority of the High Culture. There are those who truly believe it is the norm of the Nashuite Empire. And there are those who believe it is the norm because it is superior.

According to this myth, the sons of Nashua, tall, bright-eyed and bursting with energy, swept forth in an unturnable tide to swamp the universe in the name of their Emperor—honor brighten his name—because their way of life made them better than everyone they encountered.

This isn't the way things happened. Nashua did not in fact impose its power and culture on a reluctant cosmos.

People have reasons for getting together: trade, gossip, stimulation. Say that a thousand years of space travel had divided humanity—a reluctant planet might be hustled into the dirty job of putting in lines of communication and trade, and then double-shuffled into the boring routines of administration. In that case, it would be kindness to allow the planet to think of itself as an Empire.

Homage to the Emperor? Emperors are sacrificial victims. A small thing to grant them their illusions.

The superiority of the High Culture is such an illusion. In the first place, there are two "High Cultures."

The bastard High Culture that most people know is merely the tradition of Nashua, altered and simplified into a lingua franca. It provides a convenient common ground for men who need a convenient common ground. For the simple souls who mind the machinery of empire. For merchants. For that minority of mankind who in a lifetime travel from one planet to another. This High Culture touches everyone in the Nashuite Empire in at least some small way, but it is the home style of no one.

There is another High Culture. It, too, is based on the tradition of Nashua, altered and intensified. It is the native life style of a minority on Nashua, and ever smaller minorities as one travels from Nashua, until it might pertain to twenty families, or five, or one, or none. It is the High Culture of aspiration for those who never caught on to the unvoiced secret that Nashua's power is a polite fib. And it is no general norm.

Cultures are games played to common rules—for convenience. The High Culture, while not superior to very much, is a fair-to-middlin' game, and that is all.

"If you follow my advice," said Lord Semichastny,

"your first official act will be to review the Winter-Summer Laws."

Lord Semichastny was an erratic prettified prune, spry and dirty, dressed in pink silks. Well he might seek review of the Winter-Summer Laws since they had been passed specifically to encourage him to leave Delbalso. That a dozen other families were affected was an accident. Lord Semichastny might have had the grace to be ashamed, but was not.

However, Sir Henry Oliphaunt, the new Empire Administrator for Delbalso, said, "From what you give me to understand, milord, it does not seem to be a matter properly subject to Empire review."

They had impressed upon him that he should be careful in his administration, and this suited him. The position was a dull one and Sir Henry was the very man for the job. He was middle-aged, round of face, round of body, and five years married. He had accepted this position, his first for the Empire, out of a sense of duty come unexpectedly over him as an answer to his sense of finitude.

They were in the library of Lord Semichastny's country maison. The four persons present were each illuminated by a cone of light, minor illumination which Lord Semichastny said—and perhaps believed—provided them with a feeling of greater intimacy. Lady Oliphaunt's dark beauty was well set off by the soft lights that made her claim to only thirty years more reasonable than it might have seemed in another setting. The fourth person was Harbourne Firnhaber, introduced as Lord Semichastny's nephew. He was a pale, thin, well-dressed, well-mannered young man and he sat upright in a hard chair.

Lord Semichastny's summer home was set in the heart of a broad flat green farm. There were trees like furled umbrellas planted around the house and in lean graceful lines between the fields. The soil was rich and deep. The nominal crop was grass at this sod farm. The true crop, of course, was topsoil, laced together by grass roots.

There were gardens around the house, and an extensive melon patch. Lord Semichastny had a taste for melons. He raised seventeen varieties of melon, and had tasted more than a hundred of the one hundred and seventy-two varieties known to him. He was less fond of books. Of all the books he owned, he had looked at no more than twenty, and the one he read most frequently was on the subject of melons. It had one hundred and seventy-two exciting plates. Lord Semichastny thought it was a good book.

The house sat alone, without near neighbors. No one lived close enough to see or hear, though this had not kept word of Lord Semichastny and his ways from reaching the town. These matters were easier to settle in the days of banishment, plain and straight.

The house was dark, but full of noise. The mechanical staff was hard at work readying the place for Lord Semichastny's traditional end-of-the-season masquerade. They needed no light to work, and got none. They dressed the house in gay clothes, and stuffed geese with bread and rice and mushrooms. Far from leaving, Lord Semichastny was preparing the most magnificent event he had ever offered. His usual, in fact, was nothing close to magnificent. Lord Semichastny was cheap. However, he was not stupid. It made sense to him to host a masquerade and invite the new Empire Administrator and his wife. They were his house guests for the night, and in the morning Sir Henry would assume his new position.

Lord Semichastny rang the direct connection to his robot butler, Charles, again. Charles was in charge of the house. He had been designed to run this particular house, and had been uncanned here. It was his life. His peers had regard for his abilities, but thought him limited.

"Damn it, Charles, where have you been!" Lord Semichastny demanded.

"Answering the door, milord," Charles said. "May I announce Mr. Nathan Treleaven."

Lord Semichastny should have known where Charles had been. Answering the door was not a normal part of his duties. *Machines* do, *butlers* think, as Charles would have put it. Lord Semichastny assigned Charles to answer the door when he wished for some reason to humiliate him.

"Good evening, milord," said Mr. Treleaven. Mr. Treleaven was an elderly man with only one story. He had been to Nashua once in his youth—on a Wu and Fabricant Gentleman's Package Tour, though he never mentioned that—at the time of the notorious personal execution of Morgus Grimsby by the present Emperor's grandfather, who did not understand Grimsby and killed him in consequence. Mr. Treleaven had considered himself traveled ever since.

"Arrived a bit early, aren't you?" asked Lord Semichastny. "Stay here, Charles. I shall want to speak with you. Well, Treleaven, the party hasn't started yet. Do you presume on your invitation? Oh, your pardon. Sir Henry and Lady Oliphaunt. Sir Henry is the new Administrator. I was just speaking to him about the Winter-Summer Laws. And my nephew, Harbourne Firnhaber. I don't believe you've met.''

Mr. Treleaven showed his manners. Some months before his trip he had been primed by a traveling master of manners, and had used the same repertoire ever since, gradually and happily growing old-fashioned. He displayed a Dying Swan before Lady Oliphaunt.

''How like my grandfather!'' she exclaimed, very prettily and well-practiced.

Mr. Treleaven was charmed. He said that he was charmed and regretted that he would not be able to enjoy more of her company.

''You won't be attending Lord Semichastny's party?'' she asked. There was an appealing hesitation in the manner she said ''party.'' She said it as though there were two words and ended with a smile and questioning eyes.

''I think not,'' Mr. Treleaven said. ''In truth, I've not had any great taste for parties since a certain occasion many years ago on Nashua.'' That was a road to his story.

''Oh. Have you been on Nashua?''

''Not in recent years. But many years ago, I—''

''And Sir Henry Oliphaunt,'' said Lord Semichastny. ''Nathan Treleaven.''

''I believe I recognize your name,'' said Sir Henry, ''but I'm not sure of the connection.''

''Before your appointment I signed a petition addressed to your office.''

''Oh, yes,'' said Sir Henry. He set aside his book. It was a catalog of those costumes that Lord Semichastny's fac machine was prepared to deliver. Lady

Oliphaunt had already examined the catalog and found it insufficient. Sir Henry, on the other hand, had found a costume that he thought he might like. "As I was telling Lord Semichastny, I don't believe I have the authority to do as you ask. I passed your petition on."

"That is what your predecessor said." Mr. Treleaven was confirmed in his reservations about the Rock. Though he was not a native of Delbalso, he shared native opinion about the Rock and those who lived within it. Not all who labor for Empire are feckless, but if a man had a predilection for fecklessness, Mr. Treleaven felt that laboring for Empire would bring it out.

He nodded to Harbourne. "Another nephew? I'm not at all certain that we've met."

"Probably not," said Lord Semichastny. "It's an extensive family. I have any number of nephews."

This was not true, but Lord Semichastny liked to keep up appearances. He had only one nephew, and that should be enough. As the sage Aldahondo said, "One sip of wine, one morsel of bread—a lifetime of memory and meditation."

To Lord Semichastny, Mr. Treleaven said, "I'm bound from here to the Rock. My son-in-law has engaged a charterboat."

"Are you saying goodbye to them?"

"I'm saying goodbye to you. I decided on the moment to accompany them. My son-in-law and daughter and her second—a sweet girl, bless her—are all the family I have."

"You said you'd stay until the end and lend a hand in oversetting the law."

"I changed my mind."

"You said you'd come to the party. And Gramineous, too."

"No, we're going now," said Treleaven. "I'm dropping all my business and walking away. Fight your battles, Geoffrey, and when you've come away, visit us in Adeeb."

"You lack staying power," said Lord Semichastny. "Except for that single story."

"What do you mean by that?"

"Sir, you have only one story. You tell it twice an evening and I've heard it now for roundabout thirty years. It was minor when you told it first. Minor!"

"And what is it that you refer to?" asked Treleaven in some puzzlement.

"Ah, never mind," said Lord Semichastny. "A stone. A stump. Charles, throw him out."

Lord Semichastny waved at the door. Charles, obedient to this latest order, said, "Follow me, if you will, sir."

Mr. Treleaven, at the door, said, "Good evening, Sir Henry; Lady Oliphaunt; Nephew. Goodbye for now, Geoffrey."

"Goodbye," said Lord Semichastny flatly, and opened his book on melons. The picture he turned to was of a particularly succulent Divino Abbandono with green-on-gold surface and olive interior and the flavor of heaven. He had tasted a Divino Abbandono once and he found the picture a comfort.

Lord Semichastny? He was not a simple man. He heard or did not hear as it suited him. He understood or did not understand as it suited him. He had his plans and he changed them frequently. He was not above abusing his hospitality with Lady Oliphaunt on the stair—and well for him that she had not taken it to her husband. As a child he had enjoyed mud, and his taste had not altered, though his definitions had broadened.

After a moment he looked up, "Where did Charles go?" he asked.

Sir Henry said, "I believe he is seeing Mr. Treleaven to the door. By the way, I think I have the costume I want right here. This Trog costume. You see? Friendly, wouldn't you say, milord? I think it will make a proper impression. Demonstrate to everyone the excellence of my intentions."

The picture to which he pointed did present a friendly appearance. A large furry toad.

Lord Semichastny rang irritatedly for Charles. "An excellent choice, I am sure. I'll have Charles assist you."

Lady Oliphaunt had risen and begun a desultory examination of the shelves, Lord Semichastny's compounded rows of untouched books. She was joined by Harbourne Firnhaber, having explicitly and wordlessly invited him. Lord Semichastny appeared not to notice, and did notice. Sir Henry looked at them vaguely, and noticed nothing.

She said, "Tell me, Mr. Firnhaber. Will there be a party?" She asked in a low voice.

Her eye, because she had that kind of eye, had looked at him carefully. And her head, which was intermittently cool, had thought not. Times had changed and five years of secluded marriage had altered her notions of the desirable.

The noise of preparation was audible. Harbourne touched a finger to his ear and raised his eyebrows.

"Yes," she said. "But who will be there? These laws seem to be driving milord's guests away."

"A few," said Harbourne. "Isn't it fortunate that you and I aren't affected? As a transient and the wife of an Administrator, we have nothing to keep us from either traveling or staying."

He had entertained ideas himself. He recognized that he and she had much in common in their approach to life, and was consequently interested, if wary.

"Ah, at last, Charles," said Lord Semichastny. "At *last*."

"I was just answering the bell, milord."

"I told you that I wanted to talk to you, did I not?"

"Yes, milord."

"I told you to stay, did I not?"

"Yes, milord, but subsequently you ordered me to escort Mr. Treleaven to the door. And then the bell rang. I do have your order to answer it, milord."

"True," said Lord Semichastny, "but insufficient. You will simply have to learn better how to distinguish one order from another."

"Yes, milord."

"All right, Charles, grovel." Lord Semichastny rose so as better to dominate the robot. "No, no protests. No excuses. Grovel and declare your fault properly."

Charles did not grovel immediately. No protests, no excuses, but he did produce a strangled inarticulate grating sound. He rolled in a tight frustrated little circle, round and round so tightly that it was more a shimmy than a circle.

"Down, Charles. Grovel. I want the feeling of real penitence."

Lord Semichastny shook an imperative forefinger. At last, and with great reluctance, Charles flopped onto the carpet. He looked at Lord Semichastny with reproach, and then began to dig and whimper. He put no heart into it.

"Louder," said Lord Semichastny. "More feeling. And who are you, sir?" This to the young man standing in the doorway.

"Your nephew, or so I believe," the young man said. "My name is Anthony Villiers."

"I should have known, of course," said Lord Semichastny. "It's that mustache. It doesn't suit you at all. It makes you look older. If you take my advice, you'll have it off."

"Pardon, milord," said Charles from the floor. His grovels had slackened, but increased again when Lord Semichastny looked down. Voice obscured against the carpet, Charles said, "Milord, dinner is ready for service. I've just received the signal."

"All right, Charles," said Lord Semichastny. "No, don't stop. Not until I tell you. Charteris, you'll stay for dinner, of course. And there is my annual masquerade later tonight. You'll want to join in the occasion, I'm sure."

"Ordinarily, that would be so," said Villiers, "but I have pressing business elsewhere on Delbalso, Uncle."

"You'll stay to dinner, at least? We must have a talk after dinner. Family talk."

"Certainly," said Villiers. "I appreciate the invitation." He salaamed. He salaamed, kissed a proffered hand, and nodded his way around the room. He was introduced as Lord Charteris. "We must be cousins, then," he said.

"In all probability," said Harbourne. "We shall have to examine the relationship."

"Charles," said Lord Semichastny. "Up. Take Lord Charteris upstairs and allow him opportunity to ready for dinner."

With some relief, Charles raised himself from the carpet. "Yes, milord."

Before Charles reached the door, however, Lord Semichastny said, "Charles, for your transgressions, you can put on your uniform tonight and answer the door during the masquerade." And he chuckled, quite pleased with himself.

When Charles and Villiers had gone, Lord Semichastny said, "The question is which is to be master—that's all. Well, dinner is ready. Shall we go in?"

Sir Henry said, "Are we not to wait for Lord Charteris?"

"I think not. I, for one, am ready to eat. If he is prompt, he will only miss a course." It was melon, and he would not hold longer.

Sir Henry was a trifle taken aback. He was not an adaptable man, but if this was how things were done on Delbalso, he was willing to accept them for the sake of diplomacy. So he said, after a small pause, "By the way, I think you forgot to speak to the robot about my costume."

"I believe you're right," said Lord Semichastny. "Well, we'll take it up after dinner. Come along now, Sir Henry. The first course is a Bulbenko melon, and I guarantee it is better than anything you have ever eaten in your life. I selected it myself. Pulpy mellow perfection, if I do say so."

And he led Sir Henry out of the room. Lady Oliphaunt and Harbourne Firnhaber followed. Both shot looks at the stairs where Villiers had gone, both thinking their own thoughts. Lady Oliphaunt's thoughts were bright with possibility. Harbourne Firnhaber's thoughts were dark and suspicious.

Lady Oliphaunt asked, "But is there really going to be a party?"

Said Harbourne, "I believe Lord Semichastny—my uncle—is determined that there shall be. Whether there will be anybody left to come, I have no idea. I'm sure it will be more pleasant here if someone does, but perhaps more interesting if not."

Villiers walked upstairs and Charles rode a lift beside him. Both Villiers and Charles moved in the center of yellow light cones, but Villiers' light was stronger. Charles' was only a courtesy light.

The butler recognized Villiers—and not in his role of Lord Semichastny's nephew. Charles was not privy to the details of Lord Semichastny's family affairs, and curiosity in the matter was beyond him. But Charles recognized Villiers.

"Your pardon, sir," he said, "but I know you."

"Do you?" said Villiers.

"Yes, sir, I do," said Charles. "Morris, Lord Broccoli's steward, and I belong to the same club." The club was for major-domos, nominally for the exchange of household hints, but in actuality a social organization. Not everyone could join. Qualifications were required. The membership was twelve mechanicals, four humans, and a Csencsits who managed the household of a Monoprop newly rich and full of ideas. Charles was the only member on Delbalso, and that meant a good deal to him.

"I remember Morris quite well," said Villiers. He had an excellent memory. He remembered every alien he had ever met, a large percentage of the mechanicals, and even many humans.

"And he remembers you, too, sir. He has spoken warmly of you."

"Most generous under the circumstances," said Villiers. And, in fact, it was. Some months previous, an assassin searching for Villiers had dismantled Lord Broccoli's Morris in the mistaken belief that he knew Villiers' true whereabouts. An unfortunate accident.

"Between us, sir, it was the most exciting thing that ever happened to him," Charles said. "He hasn't yet stopped talking of it. I'll note your visit in the 'News and Notes' in the next issue of *Our Little Worlds*. That's our club magazine. I'm the editor. Morris will be pleased to hear of you, I'm sure."

The light chatter was a brave attempt to carry on, but at the top of the stairs, Charles stopped. His previously unspoken distress overwhelmed him. Don't think a robot can't have feelings.

He said, "I don't really enjoy that—the rolling about on the floor and declaring my fault. I was doing my job the best way I knew. It isn't fair to make me grovel."

"It did seem somewhat undignified."

"Exactly, sir. It is undignified. But I couldn't help myself, you know. He dominates me. And he'll make me wear that uniform."

That is the traditional way of masters, owners, overseers and gods. They set things for people to do, like it or not, because they have a superior grasp of how the world ought to be. They really do know best and will tell you so.

43

Villiers sympathized, adequately to his mind, inadequately to Charles', but Charles forgave him.

Villiers did not hurry himself, but only missed the melon. That was all right, because he had no particular partiality to melon—which shows that a taste for such things does not necessarily run in families. Villiers found melon too sweet for his liking, though I'm sure he wasn't so inflexible that he wouldn't have eaten melon if he had been in time for it. If he thought it was unusual that dinner had started without him, he said nothing.

The second course was soup—Delbalso borsch, made of instead-ofs, but good enough to be enjoyed for its own character. Lord Semichastny was served separately: melon soup. He was not so very erratic that he would intrude his tastes on his guests—and later in the meal he had melon relish from his own receipt—but erratic enough to serve himself what he wanted to eat. And erratic enough to press his knee against that of Lady Oliphaunt until she shifted away.

There were cones of light over every head, illuminating the company. And, again, of all the lights, that over Villiers' head was brighter than the others. That is the way the cones work.

When Villiers came in, Lord Semichastny was advising Sir Henry to have a look at the Delbalso Monist Association as a likely center of forbiddable activity. He blamed the Monist Association for the Winter-Summer Laws. Lord Semichastny broke off and advised Villiers as to his seat. Lord Semichastny was sitting at the head of the table with Sir Henry and Lady Oliphaunt on his right and left. Harbourne was seated below Sir Henry; Villiers, the other nephew, across the table, next to Lady Oliphaunt, whose chair was rather closer to him than to his uncle.

As Villiers seated himself, Lady Oliphaunt said, "Have you recent news of Nashua, Lord Charteris?" Some years before her marriage, she had had her moment on Nashua and still held news of Nashua of first importance.

Villiers said, "My agents do strive to keep my wardrobe current, but in point of fact I have not been on Nashua for three years. I'm afraid I'm sadly behind. I did hear that Prince Frederick is to be married."

"Oh, that's been dished too many times," said Lord Semichastny. "Can't we have a change of subject?"

"I take it that I'm late with the news?"

Lady Oliphaunt said, "I'm sure he could have done much better. Her family is well enough, but you would hardly call her feminine."

"To my eye," said Sir Henry, "she appears interesting."

"You've said that before," said Lady Oliphaunt. "It does seem futile to take care of one's appearance if men save their appreciation for inglorious accidents."

"Perhaps it is a sign that men's minds are as much of a puzzle to women as your minds are to us," said Villiers.

"Do you find her attractive, then, milord?"

"Interesting."

She turned to Lord Semichastny. "Do you find her attractive? I must have some support in this."

"You have my support," he said. "Of course."

Villiers said, "And you, Cousin?"

Harbourne said, "Well, Cousin, I've never met the lady, but her pictures are doubtful." He nodded to Lady Oliphaunt. "However, I am interested."

"Why?" asked Lady Oliphaunt.

"My curiosity is aroused. The lady hardly seems attractive enough to win a prince. And yet she did. I don't understand, and so I am interested. You find her attractive, Cousin, and I don't understand that. And so I am interested." He looked directly at Villiers across the table and waited for an answer.

Villiers' attention was on his dinner, and it was only after a blank moment that he looked up.

"Me, Cousin? My tastes are erratic and doubtful, and beyond explanation. I'm sure that I should properly apologize to Lady Oliphaunt. Let me assure you, milady, that the care you take with your appearance does not go unappreciated. You are an ornament to the table."

"Why thank you, milord."

Sir Henry nodded across the table at his wife. "He's right. You do very well, my dear. You look well tonight. Meant to say something about it earlier but it slipped my mind."

"Thank you, Henry," she said.

When Charles entered with the next course, Lord Semichastny said, "Sir Henry has his costume selected. After dinner you may take charge of fitting him."

"Yes, milord," said Charles.

Lord Semichastny said, "Charteris, would you like a look at our catalog of costumes?"

"No, thank you, Uncle," said Villers. "I still doubt that I shall be able to attend."

"Oh, yes," said Lord Semichastny. "I recall that you said that."

"Who will attend?" asked Lady Oliphaunt.

"I beg your pardon?" said Lord Semichastny. "I'm not sure I understand you, milady."

"What do you mean?" asked Sir Henry.

"I mean, sirs, outside of this small company, who will attend the party? These Summer-Winter Laws . . ."

"Winter-Summer." Lord Semichastny.

". . . would seem to be shortening your guest list, milord. I'm not sure that I care to make the trip to pick a costume and dress if there are to be no more than we five."

"Four," said Villiers.

"Is this true?" Sir Henry demanded, turning to Lord Semichastny in a state of mind that approached alertness.

Lord Semichastny said gently, "I've been attempting to explain the Winter-Summer Laws and their effects. It is true that many of the weaker spirits have already left the planet. Some of us, however, will endure."

"How many?"

"More than four?" asked Lady Oliphaunt.

It may have been possible that Lord Semichastny had intended to dramatize the effect of the Winter-Summer Laws by presenting Sir Henry with an absence of peers. Sir Henry, dressed in costume, waltzing in the glow of a single light cone in the middle of a dark and empty floor. Lady O tucked away and Sir Henry wandering alone in the dark. That would teach him quickly enough.

But Lord Semichastny was always ready to review his premises. "The laws will simply affect the composition of the guest list. Have no fear; I invited you to a masquerade, and there shall be one."

4

GIVEN THE RIGHT premises, any desired conclusion can be reached, automatic as addition. This is plain to most of mankind after a few years of experiment. Jumping to conclusions is an easy process, akin to cooking, which in fact it rivals in age. Pick your premises, follow the rules, and apple pie.

Jumping to conclusions is not without value. It is the core of art. But it is a dangerous business. Man entertained himself for years with notions of divinity and superiority—easy conclusions from a hundred sets of premises. The result was greater suffering than life makes necessary.

It didn't occur at first that there was a problem. Artists of the actual were too busy messing around, experimenting, to realize the results of what they did—much as a careless chef might poison thirty banquet guests through experiment gone awry. Recipes in final form are easy to follow. It is harder to invent them, and it is commonplace for men to be too close to their work for others' safety.

Once men realized the danger in false conclusions, of course they instantly reformed themselves, and as everyone knows have ever since been far more sparing in the making of them. We should all be congratulated, but the job is not yet done. Far more serious than jumping to conclusions is its antecedent—jumping to premises. The ideal man is not only sparing of conclusions, but careful about the premises to which he commits himself. Few of us are ideal, but many strive. It is another human pastime. Morgus Grimsby strove for the ideal. Even Lord Semichastny, in his own way, was a seeker of the ideal.

Every day it is possible to see the bravest and best among us reviewing their premises. We should be heartened.

Various people made their temporary excuses immediately after dinner, and Villiers and Harbourne Firnhaber were left in the library. The shelves were an untapped cache of the wisdom of the world. The books were old, of various heights and sizes and colors, filling the shelves around the room in an order carefully designed for maximum decorative effect. They were part of the original decoration of the house. Lord Semichastny had intended to line the shelves with representations, in conventional style, when by happy accident he had been able to buy a private library at a reduced price. The original catalog stood in the corner.

"Well, Cousin," said Harbourne, "will you tell me what we are in competition for? I like to know where I stand at all times."

Villiers withdrew a list from his wallet. He looked up. "You are considerably taller than I. On the other hand, I wear a mustache. For what could we possibly stand in competition? By the way, would you care to lend me your services?" He finished his examination of the list and handed it to Harbourne. "Have a look at the shelves while we talk and see if you can spot any of these titles."

Harbourne handed the list back. "There's a catalog in the corner." He pointed.

"How very convenient. Our uncle should be congratulated. I hardly expected his collection to be catalogued."

"Is your name Villiers or Charteris?" asked Harbourne. "You said Villiers. Uncle said Charteris."

"It's both," said Villiers, beginning to thumb his way through the catalog. "Or either. Villiers most of the time. Uncle did seem insistent on the title, didn't he? Perhaps to impress Sir Henry and Lady Oliphaunt?" It was non-standard cataloging, and required interpretation.

"Or to impress me," said Harbourne. "I have no title and I'm not yet ready to assume one."

"And you take me for a standard of comparison?" asked Villiers.

Before Harbourne could answer, Lady Oliphaunt entered the library. Her composure seemed shaken, but only for the fleetest moment. She set her chin, not only demonstrating spirit, but showing herself to better advantage, since her chin when lowered was not her best feature.

"Where is Sir Henry?" she asked.

"He and Charles left some few minutes ago to grapple with the fitting and production of his costume," said Harbourne. "Won't you join our company until his return, milady?"

"Thank you, Mr. Firnhaber," she said. "I believe I will." She glanced at the doorway and then crossed and sat gracefully where she could see and talk to both Villiers and Harbourne.

She said, "Have you chosen your costume, Mr. Firnhaber?"

"I have. For a time I considered growing my beard in random tufts and passing as a High-Liver of the 940's, but in the end I settled on Ian Steele."

"You shall have to assume a mustache, then," said Lady Oliphaunt.

"So much less our differences," said Villiers. "I shall assume Elaborates and match you in height, and then we shall be in competition."

"You don't mean to dress as Ian Steele?" It was a matter of importance to Harbourne. Ian Steele was his model, as he was the model for ambitious romantics everywhere, and Harbourne felt that no party should rightly sport more than one copy, and he had dibs on being that copy.

Villiers said, "Oh, no, I do not. I still doubt that I will attend the party. Affairs press. And if I do attend, I promise to forego the Elaborates."

"What about the mustache?" asked Harbourne.

Villiers smoothed the mustache. "I'm afraid that we may collide on that point, Cousin. But then a proper Ian Steele mustache should be thinner and darker, no more than two definite lines. So perhaps our collision, if it should occur, will not be that violent."

"It is a shame, Lord Charteris, that your affairs press," said Lady Oliphaunt. "Your company will be missed."

"It would seem that company is in short supply," said Villiers, "but I do thank you, madam."

"How long will you be staying?"

Villiers closed the catalog and looked up. "Long enough to speak with Lord Semichastny. My uncle and I have some small family affairs to settle."

Harbourne considered him carefully. "And then you will be leaving?" he asked slowly.

"So I intend," Villiers said. "Presently."

There was a discreet bid for attention from the doorway. A mechanical dressed in an ensemble of cleaning and polishing attachments said, "Please excuse my appearance, good gentles. I'm most heartily sorry to show you myself in this state."

"It's all right," said Harbourne. "We shall attempt to take no notice."

"Thank you, sir. I've been sent to inform you that Lord Semichastny would like to see you now in private conference."

"Who was sent for?" asked Villiers.

"Mr. Firnhaber, milord."

"Well," said Harbourne, with some satisfaction.

"Ah," said Villiers. "In that case, Cousin, we shall excuse you."

Harbourne rose from his straight-backed chair, nodded and said, "Until later."

The mechanical excused itself, rolled out of his path, and then away into the depths of the house. Harbourne's departure reduced the illumination in the room, and may well have produced some fleeting illusion of greater intimacy. Otherwise it would be hard to explain why Lady Oliphaunt, a married gentlewoman, should have spoken to Villiers in an unsuitably casual manner.

She said, "Harbourne always sits in straight hard chairs. Why do you suppose he does that?"

"On occasion, I used to do it myself," said Villiers. "I think it is due to some residual belief in the superstition that there is a relation between hard chairs and keen wits. I've ceased to believe in it myself."

"I can remember when you did," she said. In her mind, earth shifted and waters mingled. "You mean *that's* why you sat on the chair all that night, Tony?"

"I was considerably younger then," said Villiers. "Things were far more theoretical in those days and theories need testing. I believe that at one time, I had ambitions to be Ian Steele, until I tried it. And there was my vegetarian phase."

"Truly?"

"No, not truly. I have a friend who is a vegetarian. I'm not sure I care to recall the exact letter of my own particular list."

"You have changed, Tony."

"Ah, yes. The mustache. I'm not sure that I'll retain it for long."

That was not precisely what she had in mind, but she was apparently able to accept it as an appropriate approximation, for she simply smiled.

"May I ask what was causing you distress when you entered?" Villiers asked.

"Was it that obvious?"

"I would say that it was."

"Lord Semichastny—your uncle, Tony?—dropped an overripe melon at me on the stair. He blamed it on a careless mechanical and made it beg my pardon, but I'm sure it was him. We were acquainted once on Livermore, and he still presumes."

"A melon?"

"Yes. He always took delight in thinking of things to do with melons, and I believe he was attempting to remind me in indirect fashion."

Villiers said, "Yes, I do remember your acquaintances. I believe that you introduced me to several."

"Oh, yes," she said. She had the grace to blush, but her complexion was dark, her hand with cosmetics was heavy, and the lights were dim, and the gesture passed unnoticed. If we want to be aware of what people do for us, we must be alert. "I did. But Tony, it was Livermore, after all, and things just are not the same there. Sir Henry and I were married on Livermore, and that's a proper measure."

"Will you tell Sir Henry of my uncle's attempts to renew acquaintance?"

"Renew?"

"No? No."

"Tell Sir Henry?"

"No? No."

She sighed. "And to what end?"

"Is it like that?"

"Yes," she said.

"Oh," he said. "Well, I, too, have long felt that Livermore was an unusual place. I need to recover from my second visit before I attempt a third. I don't know if I owe you thanks for taking me there in the first place. I probably do. If so, you have them, Amita."

She said, "I thought you needed cheering. It was so romantic. You had just eloped with your wife to be divorced and you were such a sweet boy."

"Is that how you remember it? I hardly recognize myself."

"Oh, but you've changed, Tony—didn't we agree? And I hope you'll shave that mustache for it doesn't suit you."

Villiers touched the mustache again. "It is possible that you may be right. Perhaps I should end the experiment."

"Oh, where is my husband?" she asked with some impatience. Whatever reservations a wife may have with the married state, a husband is still a husband.

The fac machine was located with convenient proximity to Lord Semichastny's game room. Its principal use was not to supply costumes for the yearly masquerade, but rather to add an extra dimension to Lord Semichastny's occasional private parties. Where his personal pleasures were concerned, he did not skimp or scrimp. The costumes his machine produced were a redolent lot, positively guaranteed to put you firmly in character. He, his guests and relations had had many a gay romp as heroes and monsters and creatures of wonder.

Charles rolled over to Sir Henry and said, "If you will, sir, that's a uniform, not a costume."

"It looks like a costume," said Sir Henry.

The set was a green polkadotted silk sarong, a diaphanous blouse and an orange tarboosh.

"It's a uniform, and no doubt I shall be wearing it at the masquerade, sir," said Charles. He took it from Sir Henry and replaced it on its rack. "But I shan't enjoy wearing it. Now, if you'll permit me, sir, I'll take your measurements while the fac machine is cycling."

Sir Henry temporarily balanced on one foot while a measurement was taken. "What is it that you object to in your uniform?"

"Orange? Me in orange? Milord Semichastny chose orange deliberately because he knew I shouldn't like it."

This seemed loose talk to Sir Henry, extremely loose. It is all very well to give robots Limited Volition, but not if it is going to be abused.

"Pardon me, sir," said Charles, and dialed for the Trog suit. "I think you made an excellent choice, sir. This costume—Lord Semichastny himself wore it at a party last year. Mrs. Armbruster was Semiramis Among the Doves."

Sir Henry said, "See here! There is a natural order in things. If Lord Semichastny picked your uniform, I'm sure that he had a very good reason in mind, and it isn't your place to question his judgment. I find my Presentation Uniform unsightly, but if they ordered me to wear it, I would. You should do the same. Smile through."

That is, this is what he intended to say. In actual fact, before he was much past "natural order," the machine began to produce the Trog costume and distracted his attention, and consequently a certain amount of conviction and force was lost. The suit was of gray shading to olive. And to Sir Henry's eye, the great lolling empty head spoke of all the friendliness and good intentions one could ask for. "Smile through" was no better than a mumble.

"My word," he said. "That is fine."

"So Mrs. Armbruster thought," said Charles. "She gave me a dove to keep. May I help you into the costume, sir?"

The costume swallowed Sir Henry exactly, so fine were Charles' measurements and the machine's ability to suit. Anyone who did not know a Trog at first hand—which is to say, nearly everyone—might easily think him one. A telltale sign were his eyes. The eyes of a genuine Trog are a divine and lumined blue. Sir Henry's eyes were lumined and blue, but lacked the true sparkle of divinity. But not everyone would be able to catch him on that, lacking first-hand experience of Trogs.

"This is marvelous," Sir Henry said. "I shall have to show Lady Oliphaunt."

His voice was somewhat muffled because he hadn't yet mastered the controls of the suit. It was quite an engineering marvel. With practice, one could work the controls and walk and talk and pass for a genuine Trog. The suit had sanitary features and a snack shelf and reservoirs for as many as five drinks. A cheaper version of the suit only had one reservoir, but Lord Semichastny and personal pleasures . . . Sir Henry said, "Show Lady Oliphaunt," over and over until his voice came clear.

He waltzed a little circle to see if he could, quite forgetting himself and his proper dignity as the hand of the Emperor in this sad corner. Or it may have been the final carefree moment before the assumption of his responsibilities. In any case, it was a mistake. Creatures with Limited Volition should be treated with consistent reserved distance lest they be confused and misled into overstepping themselves.

Perhaps it was the influence of the suit. It may be that the well-known weirdness of Trogs, sufficient in prime to make their restriction reasonable, is a direct result of their form. At least pause to consider that if you looked like that, it would probably affect your mind. And to wear a Trog suit may be to open the susceptible mind to a metapsychotic transference. In any case, Trog suits are illegal on thirteen worlds on general principles.

Charles, presented with the waltzing Trog, misguidedly said, "I find it impossible to smile through, sir. I truly hate to grovel and wear orange."

"What?"

"Grovel—as before dinner."

"Oh, yes, that." Sir Henry thought. "But then we don't always like what is good for us, do we? I think you should accept Lord Semichastny's judgment, even if you don't understand it. If you will only accept the principle of natural order, you will find that life becomes much easier to deal with. Smiling is the major part."

Charles said, "Were positions reversed, would you smile?"

"I think I would. I'm sure I would."

"In that case, sir, grovel. And enjoy it." Limited Volition can be a dangerous thing. An audacious challenge.

But Sir Henry the Trog fell to consideration of the suggestion. And since he did accept the principle of natural order, he thought he could. Or ought to be able to. "All right," he said.

Sir Henry levered himself to the floor, paused on his knees for a breath, and then he began to kick and whimper.

"Louder," said Charles inexorably. "And you're supposed to yell your fault."

"My fault! Oh, my fault! I am sorry. I repent. Forgive me. (What is it I did?) Whatever I did, I'm sorry for it and if you'll only forgive me I'll never do it again."

Finally Charles said, "All right. That's enough."

Sir Henry came back to his knees.

"Did you enjoy it?" asked Charles.

59

"I'm smiling," said Sir Henry, who was a bit winded. It was impossible to say whether or not he actually was smiling because of the costume. But if he did smile, perhaps he did smile. It wasn't impossible that he should. After all, in spite of all Charles said, deep within him, deep deep within him, he did enjoy groveling just the least little bit.

"Yes, sir," said Charles.

Sir Henry said, "I'll have to speak to Lord Semichastny. At close range your carpets are quite lovely." The heavy Trog head nodded. "But that can wait. I must have my word with Lady Oliphaunt."

"Yes, sir," said Charles.

"I trust that was satisfactory?"

"Yes, sir," said Charles.

"Very good, then. Keep smiling."

Sir Henry clumped out and down the corridor. He may have been smiling. At the least, he did offer every appearance of friendliness and good intention. Assume he was smiling—as a man who has taken the dangerous step of testing his premises, and then found them true, he had reason. Be heartened.

Harbourne skirted a mess on the stairs. The mechanical who had carried the message was cleaning it up.

"What happened here?" Harbourne asked.

"An accident," the mechanical said. And then, "It was a melon. It was my fault."

"I'm sure it was," said Harbourne.

Harbourne was ambitious and able. He had thought about what he wanted in life, and through self-discipline and sacrifice he was slowly achieving what he coveted, slowly molding himself into what he wanted to be. He was cool and played his hand warily.

Lord Semichastny, on the other hand, was less concerned with what he might be. He knew himself for what he was and didn't care if he pleased anyone. He did as he pleased and spoke as he pleased. He even dressed more extravagantly than Harbourne.

The room was all hung about with ornamental rugs. Long-pile, short-pile, fringed. They made the walls close and the room dark and warm.

Lord Semichastny invited Harbourne to take a seat and Harbourne sat down in a hard straight chair. Lord Semichastny remained standing, free to prowl as he pleased, the room his run.

"Aren't you taking a chance in leaving Villiers alone with Lady Oliphaunt?" Harbourne asked. "She's restless. He's attractive, isn't he? It appeared to me that you were trying to fix your interest."

"Why thank you," said Lord Semichastny dangerously. "But you underestimate me, Harbourne. Lady Oliphaunt and I are friends of long standing, and my interests are already fixed. Young Charteris will not be here for long, whatever his attractions."

"Is the title genuine?" Harbourne asked.

"Yes," said Lord Semichastny. "Are you jealous? Some nephews have better endowments than others, but this one is my sister's son and comes by his title honestly."

Harbourne was jealous. But he said, "Sister's son?"

"To be sure. Did you think him in common trade?"

Harbourne said, "If I had a title, I would go to Nashua now. I wouldn't wait any longer."

There are many aspirant gentlemen on shelves around the Empire, ripening themselves for Nashua like so many cheeses. Harbourne felt himself almost ready, but still lacked the resolve to go. The thought of Nashua awed him.

"Enter a game. Fight for a title."

"I don't fight that well."

"You might buy one. I myself have several minor titles that I could part with. How would you like to style yourself Thegn of Vrane?"

"I'm not sure," said Harbourne. "I fear your prices, milord."

"If my sources of information are correct, you have already booked passage from Delbalso."

"After your party, milord. I had meant to tell you. With winter approaching, I thought it might be appropriate to visit another of my widespread family."

Lord Semichastny circled the room. He lurked as he talked. From behind Harbourne, he said, "It's a pity you have no taste for winter sports. How would you like to be Thegn of Vrane? Would you stay the winter for it?"

Harbourne considered. "I think I might."

"Well, it's unfortunate that I no longer hold the title. If I did, I'm more than certain that I would test your resolve. On the other hand, you are planning to leave."

"Yes," said Harbourne, trying to suppress his frustration. Turning on a hard wooden chair to speak over your shoulder can remind you where you are and who you are.

"Would you like a good recommendation to carry away with you, one speaking highly of your ability and initiative? Full credit for a splendid job as overseer of my Delbalso estates."

"Is this another hypothetical bargain, or do you mean it?"

"Oh, I do mean it. Of course I mean it. I'm surprised to hear that you have doubt of me." Lord Semichastny paused behind his desk and put his hands behind his back and looked directly at Harbourne. "I merely want you to go into town and find typical Delbalso natives, a good representative sample, and invite them out here to the masquerade. If it can't be done any other way, let us show Sir Henry the company he can expect."

"The Monist Association, too?"

"Oh, yes. Them in particular. Dig them out, bring them to the light, and let us give Sir Henry the chance to see them, whatever they are."

Harbourne took a heavy breath and nipped at an irritation on his lip, and then he said, "But I know no one."

"What?" said Lord Semichastny. "Here this long and still a stranger? In any case, Nephew, I have no interest in inviting your acquaintances to the masquerade. I want people you don't know and would no longer care to. The reference, after all, speaks of—what did I say?—initiative and ability."

"Yes," said Harbourne. "That's what you said. All right. I'll do it, but under the condition that I have a hand in drafting the recommendation."

"Of course," said Lord Semichastny. "Who other than you knows your unique and particular talents so well?"

And so they came to terms. But Lord Semichastny could not resist saying, "You might be interested to know that my nephew—my *other* nephew—passed himself by his family name when he made his bow on Nashua.''

'' 'Villiers'?''

"Yes. And he managed, or so I'm given to understand.''

"I believe this may be your husband now, milady,'' said Villiers.

Sir Henry the Trog pranced into the room, humming, casting fantastic shadows on the wall. This was not the terror-arousing disintegration of character that it might appear. It was, in fact, another risk-taking exploration of the possibilities of Sir Henry's new body. He was one with Icarus. But he frightened his wife. Daedalus got scared, too.

"Is that you, Henry?'' she asked.

"Indeed it is,'' he said. "And a very good evening to you. Tell me, Lord Charteris, what think you of my choice of costume?''

"It fits you admirably,'' said Villiers.

"That was Charles' doing. And between us, he has some very loose ideas for a robot. I demonstrated natural order to him, however, and he may be the better for it. What's the matter, my dear?''

"Nothing,'' she said. "You disconcerted me for a moment.''

"Oh,'' he said, and the almost blue-enough eyes bulged pensively.

"As it happens,'' said Villiers, "I've had occasion to observe a Trog in nature, and your representation is largely excellent, Sir Henry.''

"Really?'' asked Sir Henry. "They're—I mean, we're—restricted, aren't we?''

"You are," said Villiers. "But then I travel widely."

"Do you think you could show me what I'm doing wrong?" asked Sir Henry."

"To be sure," said Villiers, and his light cone shone a little brighter.

Lady Oliphaunt gave an exasperated sigh and sat down with her back to them. If there was a flaw in her character—an unfortunate thing to suggest even tentatively of such a pretty lady—it was that she lacked patience. A failure to appreciate Trogs cannot be called a character flaw. It has to be called a lapse in taste. Oh, well, she was still an attractive woman, if not as attractive as she had been, say, five years before. Five years before, Villiers might have been a shade less interested in demonstrating how a Trog walks. But then, people change.

A mechanical serving table wheeled in while Villiers had Sir Henry doing hunkers and squats.

"My word, this is difficult."

"But I assure you that it's typical behavior. It's easier to do for a natural Trog."

The serving table made a slow graceful curve across the room, pirouetting as it came, raising and lowering its serving covers with the rhythm of an elegant bird. Having demonstrated itself to best advantage, it came to a halt before Villiers.

"Milord," it said, "Lord Semichastny awaits your attendance."

Villiers said, "Your pardon, Sir Henry. I'm stayed for."

."Go, by all means," said Sir Henry the Trog. "I shall practice what you have shown me until I see you again."

When Villiers and the serving table, still fluttering its serving covers, had left the library, Sir Henry did a final practice hunker.

Then he said, "Well, my dear, isn't this a fine costume? I'm liking it more by the minute. Don't you think it radiates friendliness and good intentions?"

"To be frank, Henry," she said, "I don't. Trogs are such uncertain creatures."

"Are they?" he asked. "Uncertain." It gave him something to think about, since as it happened he was feeling rakishly uncertain at that particular moment, and it made him aware and gave him pause for enjoyment.

But then he said, "And . . . but . . . what do you know of Trogs, my dear?"

"When I was presented on Nashua, I met the Trog Chief Hostage. He was a soldier, black and white, and very fierce. He gave me a considerable fright."

"Do I frighten you?" Sir Henry asked.

"I must confess you don't," she said.

"Oh."

"However, when you entered you did disconcert me for a brief moment," she said, allowing her face to break.

"I'm sorry," he said automatically, and moved to comfort her as she cried briefly. He comforted her with a clumsiness that clearly showed his need for further practice in the costume.

Lady Oliphaunt said, "Henry, will you take the suit off now?"

"Not yet, my dear. I'm still getting used to it."

She sat up abruptly, glancing off his muzzle with some force. She rose. She said, "I'll be going into town later to see if I can find an appropriate costume for this masquerade."

"Oh," he said. "I'm disappointed. I was rather hoping I could persuade you to make a set with me."

You see now, perhaps. You couldn't tell a man like that about a melon on the staircase.

There was something that seemed familiar in the serving table's manner and Villiers wondered about it. "Excuse me," he said. "Did you bring the message for Mr. Firnhaber earlier in the evening?"

The table closed all its covers. "I was hoping you wouldn't recognize me, milord. Those are my least attractive attachments."

"I wouldn't say that at all," said Villiers. "But I must congratulate you. I think you make a most attractive serving table."

When Villiers entered, Lord Semichastny dismissed the table and offered him a choice of hard or soft chair. Villiers waited until Lord Semichastny had drawn out his own seat behind the desk, and then he took the soft chair and settled into it comfortably. He accepted a smoke with the confidence of a man who has no fear of befuddling his mind, and doesn't mind greatly if he fouls his lungs. That's nonchalance. Lord Semichastny lit up, too, so as not to be overtopped.

Lord Semichastny had a stack of letters on the desk before him. He squared the pile.

He said, "I'm curious to know what possessed your father to send you my way?"

Villiers said, "I'm afraid I can't answer that. I'm on no better terms with him than you are. He has a peculiar sense of humor. He may have just been curious to see what we would make of each other. For myself, I haven't so many relatives not to enjoy the chance of meeting one.'' He blew out smoke.

Lord Semichastny thumbed the letters, flipping them over one by one. He said, ''I've seen mention of you from time to time in the Garlinghouse *Alumni Notes*.''

''I remember seeing mentions of you, sir. Class of '09, I believe. My address has been unstable of late, and I seem to have missed the *Notes*, though I must admit, not greatly.''

''You, too?'' asked Lord Semichastny. ''When I left the place I promised that I would never go back, and I never have. Well, I think we understand each other well enough. I like you, Nephew. I had expected you younger and without that mustache.''

''More like my picture in the *Alumni Notes?*''

''Well, perhaps so. But you'll do. How would you like to stay here over the winter? You might want to take a shot at serving as my overseer. How does that sound? I have the feeling that these aren't altogether prosperous times for you.'' Lord Semichastny pulled a letter out from the stack and placed it on top, and then began flipping through the stack, top to bottom, again.

Villiers said, ''I think not, sir. I have my own affairs to pursue. Besides, I understood the Winter-Summer Laws to be a tax on you. Will you still be here at the end of the winter?''

''That particular game is as yet unsettled,'' said Lord Semichastny. ''I have more resources than the anonymous mob gives me credit for. Will you give me a good hand and stay through the masquerade?''

''I regret to have to say it, Uncle, but affairs do press me. I have need of the money I believe you to hold for me.''

"Money? Did you expect to come by money here?"

"My father directed me here for it."

"We did agree that your father has a notorious sense of humor."

"Have you mail for me?"

"Mail? I don't recall any."

Villiers said, "You expected my coming."

"Oh, yes. There must have been something." Lord Semichastny began the most earnest of hunts through the pile of letters in his hands, examining each letter with scrupulous care lest anyone accuse him of making less than the best of searches. At last he stopped, some halfway through the pile, and produced a particular letter. "Why, here we are!" he exclaimed in surprise. "It's well you reminded me. It's for you."

He handed the missive across the desk to Villiers. It was addressed to him in care of Lord Geoffrey Semichastny and it had been opened. It was not a letter in any proper sense. It was an itinerary. The itinerary was a list of places that Villiers' father and brother intended to be, so that Villiers could better avoid them. That was what the money was for. But there was no money.

"And there was no money with this?" Villiers asked.

"I'm sorry," said Lord Semichastny. "If you expect it, I'm sure it will turn up shortly. Probably after the masquerade. To while the time, you might pick out a costume when you wake."

When Villiers left Lord Semichastny's presence, he went immediately downstairs to the library and stole a book. He walked deliberately into the library and took a book, not intending to return it, and hopelessly marring the symmetry of the shelves for any close observer. He only took one book because there was only one book he wanted.

On his way upstairs, he encountered Sir Henry on the first landing. Sir Henry was still in his Trog suit.

Sir Henry said, "I find stairs difficult. They take practice."

"You are doing excellently," said Villiers.

"By the way," said Sir Henry. "Am I right in remembering that the color of my coat is meaningful?"

"I believe you are. If I am right, you are an agrarian gentleman."

"A squire, so to speak?"

"So to speak," said Villiers.

On the second landing, Villiers encountered Harbourne Firnhaber.

"Good evening, Cousin. About to do some bedtime reading?"

"I believe I will," said Villiers.

Harbourne fixed him with a firm eye. "Is it true that you made your bow on Nashua under your family name instead of your title?"

Villiers regarded him for a moment. At last he said, "I'll tell you what, Cousin. I'll trade you question for question. Fair enough?"

"I suppose. What is your question?"

"What is your mother's address?"

Harbourne blushed. Under his soft cone of light it was a very pretty effect. "I've changed my mind," he said, and plunged away.

On the third landing, Villiers met Lady Oliphaunt.

"Shh, Tony," she said. "I'm going into town later

after a costume. Meet me and we will talk privately."
And she pressed a slip of paper into his hand.

Before he could fairly respond, something whizzed
by their heads down the central stairwell, just missing
their balustrade, and smashing rottenly on the next
floor below. Villiers was startled.

"What was that?" he said.

"That was a melon," she whispered, and slipped off
down the hall.

Sir Henry, using the full power of his suit's resources, which were considerable, called up from below, "And what is this, now?"

Lord Semichastny's voice yelled angrily from the
floor above: "Damned prank-playing robot!" There
was an appropriate clanking and scurrying. "Charles!
Where are you, Charles?"

Villiers yawned, for it had been an extremely long
day for him. He wandered off down the hall toward his
room, examining the book he had taken. It was *Companions of Vinland* by Ottilie A. Liljencrantz.

Before he went to bed, he prepared the book for
mailing. When he was done, he crawled under the
covers. The cone of light was still shining over his
head, carefully adjusting itself not to shine in his eyes.

"Turn off, please," Villiers said.

The light turned off.

5

MONISM promises only one thing: to make you very very happy. There is a catch, of course. To be happy as a Monist, you must accept Monist definitions of happiness. If you can—and many do—you have a blissful life before you. Congratulations.

The Monists—in the single person of a Meditation Leader named Coppersmith—came to Delbalso in 1430. He rented a small building, began to talk to people, and let the general observe his sunny personality. If anyone asked, he credited Monism. After a year, he had converted his landlord, Stanley Joralemon, to the Monist Way, the landlord had turned all his considerable worldly possessions over to the commonality, and Joralemon House was a-building.

When Gideon Coppersmith left Delbalso five years later to carry the blessings of Monism to yet another world—his fourth—there were two active, thriving

Houses in the Delbalso Monist Association. Less than thirty years later, there were four: Joralemon, Schermerhorn, Montague and Pierrepont. Joralemon and Pierrepont were talking of sponsoring another House—Joralemon's third daughter, Pierrepont's first. It would be located somewhere outside the town. Sentiment favored the name "Coppersmith House."

You may ask those who live in Joralemon, Schermerhorn, Montague and Pierrepont, and they will all tell you that they are very happy. And they are, of course, because they believe they have every reason to be. It's built into the system.

Still, for an illusion . . .

It is indisputable that Monist children are bigger, stronger and healthier than the Delbalso average. And they smile more. There is a study from the Petenji Institute that says they do.

Monist business enterprises prosper. Monist art is counted an ornament. A Monist is I-go champion of Delbalso.

Perhaps the Monists aren't really happy. Still, it is a fact that in less than thirty-five years, "happy as a Monist" has replaced "merry as a grig" in Delbalso popular idiom, so someone thinks Monists are happy.

Slyne prowled. Through his mind curled fancies of himself as Nemesis, a dark and midnight destroyer. His body bent low. His amplifiers were open to the full. Since he lacked formal introduction to the Trog, he had to follow intuitive patterns, gross assumptions, and problematic possibilities through the night streets. It was all very uncertain. McBe trailed behind on faith alone.

In time, Slyne's amplified possibilities and McBe's faith brought them both to a great enclosing wall. There were gates in the wall, but Slyne passed them by. Then the wall connected to a building, and there were doors. Slyne stopped in front of one of the doors. A banner with a blue motif hung above it.

"What is this building?" McBe asked. "Is it a university?" By making a special effort, he had retained the information that the Trog they sought was a scholar and hence might be found in company with knowledge.

"No," said Slyne. "It's a House of the Delbalso Monist Association."

McBe blanched and gasped. "A Monist House?" He rolled his eyes.

"Come, come," said Slyne. "No fits and starts, McBe."

"We're not going to go in there, are we?"

Slyne said, "Brace yourself, McBe."

Reluctantly, McBe went into a brace. "Sir."

"What is your primary sense?"

"Sir?"

"Which of your senses do you customarily rely on?"

"Eyesight, I suppose, sir, in the light."

"By all means, then, McBe, look about you. Very slowly."

McBe slowly looked about him. The street was a gentle curve, faintly lit. There were lights at various places in the great building, and lights above the doors. There was a dark sway of foliage in the breeze.

"Do you see anything that can harm you?"

"No, sir. But it's dark."

"What's your next best sense?"

"Smell, I suppose."

He spoke doubtfully, and well he might. As a self-protective device, all his senses were filtered so that he shouldn't be swamped by more data than he could safely handle. His hearing was miserable. Almost anything could be said in his presence, short of his name, and pass unheard. For him to hear music, it had to be loud enough to annoy. He would turn it on for a time, let it irritate him and his neighbors, and then turn it off again, convinced that it must have purgative value, since he could detect none other. He had a regular time marked on his schedule.

Most people, asked their second sense, would say hearing. McBe's hearing was impugned every day. His sense of smell was no better, but no one had had occasion to challenge it.

No matter—he pleased Slyne. Slyne wanted to come close and whuffle, but he restrained himself.

He said, "Take a good deep breath. Taste the air. Sample it carefully." He took his own advice and caught the faintest intoxicating whiff of McBe.

McBe took a shocking lungful of air. He held it in and then he let it dribble out. Anxious to justify his own estimate, he sampled the Night.

"Well," said Slyne, "anything harmful?"

"No," said McBe. "But it tastes wild." He suppressed a shudder.

"What sense next?"

"Hearing?" asked McBe.

"All right. Listen. What do you hear?"

McBe listened. He not only listened, he continued to see and smell. He heard only the sound of the wind. He saw nothing. He smelled vague wild promise. It gave him the sense that there were things lurking just beyond the limit of his ability to detect them.

"I don't hear anything, sir."

"Of course not. Now expand yourself. There's nothing out here you can't dominate. Feel your size. Feel your strength. Take power from your uniform."

But McBe took no sense of power from his uniform. He hadn't gotten past expanding his senses, and the accumulation of strange dark impressions was too much for him.

Between tightly clenched teeth, he said, "I believe you may be right, sir. I think we could go inside now, if you like."

"Very good," said Slyne, inhaling. "I thought all you needed was a little encouragement. Very soon you'll be out here planetside all the time, eh, Mc-Be?"

"I'm sure you're right," McBe said, watching him sound the door of the Monist Association. Imagine— to be feeling relief to be allowed within a Monist Association. But then those big walls can fence out the wild world as well as guard secrets.

As they waited for the door to open, McBe said, "Do you think they'll let me use their sanitary facilities?" He was delicate about the things he said.

"Is it that time again?" Slyne asked.

McBe nodded. That was easier than an explanation. This foray into the darkness had thrown him completely off schedule and he had the feeling that almost anything was possible. Anyway, he knew he had to use a toilet, schedule or no.

A Warder answered the door. He little more than blinked at the Empire uniforms or at Slyne, who was not usual. "Yes?" he said.

McBe said, "May I use your bathroom?" And he looked over his shoulder at the Night.

"Well, I suppose you may," the Warder said. "Come on inside. Around there to the right, second door."

He pointed McBe on his way. The floor was parquetry. The walls were paneled in wood.

Slyne said, "We have reason to believe that a Trog came to this House tonight. To this very door." His nose twitched as he sought to know the Warder better.

"Not as far as I know," the Warder said.

"We wish to examine its papers."

"Is that your job, examining papers?"

"For the most part."

"Then I can understand your wanting to examine the papers of a Trog. I'm sure they must be special and exciting. Fully as gaudy as your own."

"Less."

"Is that so? But why do you search here—in a Monist Association—and, in particular, why, when your authority does not stretch beyond the door to the Rock?"

"You are right, of course, Reverend Sir. I have no . . . particular authority. Particular authority . . ." He mulled the phrase and found it good. "But this is not an official investigation."

"You're wearing your uniform," the Warder pointed out quite reasonably.

"An accident," said the Orthodoxou. "I forgot to change before venturing out."

"And your friend?"

"He neglected to change as well. But it is of no moment. We simply wish to know whether a Trog has been here tonight."

The Warder considered. "All right. I'll check, though I don't know why I should." He rang the House Plexus. "Walt, has a Trog been in the House tonight?" He nodded. "Oh. Yes. No, two I.S.ers from the Rock. That's what *I* said. Oh—Badrian."

McBe entered, looking over his shoulder with an air of puzzlement, as the Warder turned back. McBe looked up just in time to avoid a collision. McBe bobbed politely.

"Thank you," he said, and rubbed his fingers publicly to show that they were clean and dry.

The Warder nodded. To Slyne, he said, "Your Trog was here but he left some time ago."

"Why was he here?" Slyne asked sharply.

The Warder looked reproachful. "But, sir, this isn't an investigation. Do you fail to recall?"

Slyne nodded reluctantly. "I do recall," he said.

"I may tell you that he left by Gate Three."

"Will you show us the way?" Slyne asked.

"Oh, I'm afraid I can't," said the Warder. "I can't leave my post and there is no one else to show you. You'll have to find your own way around the outside. It's about the same distance either way."

"Very well," said Slyne. "Come along, McBe."

"Already?" said McBe.

"Pull yourself together, McBe. Good night, sir."

"Good night," said McBe.

"Good night," said the Warder. "Oh, one thing. The Xochitl Sodality is playing Wonders and Marvels tonight. You had better be careful. They may take you for a Marvel." And he closed the door.

McBe didn't hear, of course. Slyne heard, but didn't know what the Warder meant. He didn't ask McBe.

McBe shot a look at the Night and then lowered his sight to his feet and the street. He inclined his head. "You should see what they do in there," he said. His tone was a mixture of awe and puzzlement. He told what they did in there.

Slyne found it strange, but no stranger than the ordinary run of human behavior. He found it less strange than McBe did, and he found it less strange than he found McBe.

But McBe was puzzled and expected an answer. When you are surrounded by a strange and hostile world, you need answers.

"I take it to be essentially religious," said Slyne, considering this to be a safe answer.

"Religious," said McBe. "But that would make it all right, then." McBe had respect for religion.

"If it's religious, then it's all right?" Slyne asked, perking behind his amplifiers.

"Why, yes. I suppose," said McBe.

"Very interesting," said Slyne. His damp little nose behind its lattice touched McBe's ear. Slyne whuffled deeply. He tried to make it last, but like all good holy experiences, this one, too, was ephemeral. A holy experience, infinitely extended, becomes trivial. Understanding this, Slyne exhaled and set off around the palisade for Gate Three. And McBe trailed behind, swiping at his ear.

"I have a special responsibility for young Badrian," said the man. His name was Ossian Chimmeroon. He was newly come to white-mantled maturity and still settling into his new set of relationships, but enjoying the feeling of being a sage. The blue trimming on his white robes indicated Joralemon House. "Not only am I his Guide Leader, but he bought up my place in the Xochitl Sodality. Besides, I should be able to guide you as well as anyone you care to name. If anyone can tell you where Xochitl will run, it's me."

He walked the quiet winding curve of street. Beside him padded Torve the Trog. Chimmeroon had offered to take Torve to Badrian Beaufils since it was Xochitl Sodality Night and Badrian was out playing in the streets.

The town was a bowl, with a green and gardens in the cup curve and the quarters of the town laid out on the slopes above. People were settled in for the night. Houses were dark. The streets were private. From time to time as they walked there were vantages from which could be seen the crystal sprawl of the city. There was a breeze that toyed lightly with sound and temperature, rustling and flickering. It was a pleasant evening for a walk.

"Is a nice planet you have here," said Torve the Trog.

"Thank you. We like it," said Chimmeroon. Of course, since he had never been off the planet, he had nothing to compare it with. Nonetheless, it is a fact that he liked Delbalso.

Now is the opportunity to observe the difference between a genuine Trog and a gross impostor. Even in dim light, even in darkness. Torve's eyes shone a genuine divine lumined blue. Otherwise there wasn't a great deal of obvious difference.

Above them, cracking and flashing white lightnings, a ship descended slowly toward the Rock. There were beacons on the rim of the Rock that marked its dark flatulent bulk against the sky. Chimmeroon and Torve the Trog turned to watch until lightnings and beacons merged in flaring white and flashing red. Then the crackle and flash ended. The beacons continued to wink imperturbably, and yellow afterimages danced on their eyes.

Torve continued to stare at the Rock.

"Imagine that's the nightboat from Duden," said Chimmeroon.

Torve squatted. "I have feeling of imminent conjugation," he said. "Pardon. I must steep myself." He closed his eyes and went away. He concentrated with the solemn gravity of an old man examining his excreta for portents. After a silent minute or more, he made his throbbing noise, *"Thurb."* He made it again, a number of times.

This was art, an aid to his concentration. And there, of course, is your essential difference—not the gross duplicable exterior, but the Troggish heart. That cannot be chunked out by a machine.

Torve's art continued for its own sake after its utile function was complete. Torve paused for a brief moment to savor the event. Then he rose.

"Yes," he said. "No mistake. Imminent conjugation."

It is this sort of concept that is in part responsible for the restriction of Trogs. What can be fruitfully exchanged, after all, with people who believe that events ripen themselves, bide their time, wait for the proper interactive moment to occur? At a moment of conjugation, as Torve would have it, a cluster of events burgeon to their mutual satisfaction. And through the morass of events, things—Trogs and humans and dogs and bricks and sticks—must take their own chances. Events will use them as they will, and the best one can do is swim with the tide.

This representation is gross and inaccurate, of course, but still it would not be unfair to say that Torve considered himself largely irrelevant to his *thurbs*, which left him free to enjoy them to a degree that would be disgraceful in a human artiste.

Chimmeroon asked, "And what is 'imminent conjugation,' Friend Trog?"

Torve explained at some length, speaking of lines of occurrence and other inadequate approximations. He molded air with his furry fingers by way of illustration. Chimmeroon understood hardly a word. Some philosophies are not easily exported. Villiers and Torve had traveled together considerably, and neither would claim to understand the other, so Chimmeroon cannot be blamed.

Chimmeroon did become convinced that "imminent conjugation" was not so rare an event in the Trog's experience that he should have reason for alarm, and after a more than reasonable show of attention, he nodded his lack of understanding and changed the subject. He reached beneath his robes and produced a handsome box of trocchi wood graced by inlaid filigree. He flipped it open with a practiced thumb.

"Majoon?" he said.

There was a row of neat candies within—honey and nuts, and wondrous spices, all dipped in toasted sesame seeds. Chimmeroon took one and offered the box.

"In surety," said the Trog, taking three. Or would it be fair to say that three pieces forced themselves upon him? In any event—three.

Chimmeroon nibbled his piece with proper respect, for majoon deserves respect, but the Trog had all three pieces in his mouth before Chimmeroon had replaced his box beneath his burnoose, and had gobbled and gulped the lot before Chimmeroon was more than begun. Ah, but it is futility to expect politeness from a Trog, or a proper appreciation of a careful blend of delicate flavourings.

Torve did smile widely. "Is good," he said. "Already I feel seeping emanations." It was almost as though the pleasure he took was not so much in the eating as in the digestion of the candy.

Chimmeroon may have marveled at this, but as an officially wise old man—even if only newly so—he was willing to grant the Trog his peculiarities. For Badrian Beaufils' sake, if none other. And, as they walked, digestion proceeding, the Trog's smile grew broader.

However, Chimmeroon was not given an extended opportunity to observe the process. Before they had progressed more than a few blocks down the sloping, winding street toward the green center of town, a party of four men came out of a side street and hailed them.

Chimmeroon groaned. "Newman, Rose, Zimmerman and Cohen," he said. "I hope they don't insist on singing."

The four were of Chimmeroon's age, or a bit younger—mature men. They were dressed in green, with little peaked and jaunty caps. One had a feather in his cap.

"They sing?" asked Torve.

"Oh, yes," said Chimmeroon. "At every sodality meeting. And badly." Having been named Ossian, from an early age he had looked upon poetry and song as being particularly his own and felt free to criticize as he would. If he had not criticized Torve's attempts, it was largely because he had not recognized them as art.

"Well, how are things over at Pierrepont House?" Chimmeroon asked as the four came up.

"Well enough," said the one with the feather. "What are you doing out tonight, Ossian? You know this is Xochitl's night. You have your new sodality. Can't you let go?"

"We're just looking for Badrian Beaufils," said Chimmeroon. "This is a pen pal of his. Torve the Trog—Xavier Newman." And he introduced the others—Rose, Zimmerman and Cohen. They nodded without enthusiasm. In fact, they seemed to be regarding Chimmeroon with outright suspicion. How they looked at Torve was something else again.

"This is the outside of enough, Chimmeroon," said Newman. "You don't think we're going to allow you to hand over a Marvel like this to Joralemon House, do you?"

"But I'm not *playing*," said Chimmeroon in exasperation.

"But we *are*," said Zimmerman. "It is our night and this is our territory. Finders keepers, Chimmeroon."

Torve just smiled broadly. *"Thurb,"* he said.

"Oh, my," said Rose. "That's it. He has to be our Marvel. None of the other Houses will have anything to compare."

"But he's just Badrian Beaufils' pen pal," said Chimmeroon.

"Come now," said Newman with no sign of belief. "You were a Xochitl long enough to know a proper Marvel when you see one."

"Can you really write?" asked Cohen.

Torve nodded.

The four moved around the Trog and looked at Chimmeroon. Chimmeroon banged his knuckles together and looked pensively at them all. "Do you understand what this is about?" he asked the Trog.

"Of course," said Torve. "Is imminent conjugation."

"Oh," said Chimmeroon. "Well, then. Go along with these gentlemen—such as they are—and I will do my best to find Badrian Beaufils, Friend Trog."

"Do that," said Newman. "He can find us on the green when it's time to match Marvels."

"All right," said Chimmeroon. "All right." He drew his gaberdine and his dignity about him, and turned away down the street.

The four continued to stand close about the Trog.

Rose said, "Let's show the others what we've found."

Zimmerman said, "I think we had best be on our way before Chimmeroon finds Badrian Beaufils."

Cohen said, "He was mad, wasn't he?"

Newman said, "Well, come along, Trog. Friend Trog."

Torve said, "You sing, is true?"

"Why yes," said the four.

6

Do PLACES dream of people until they return?

"Turn on, please," Villiers said, but only at last
when he had searched on hands and knees without
success for the copy of *Companions of Vinland* that he
had prepared for mailing before he went to sleep.

The light roused when he did. Villiers swung out of
bed and yawned and stretched, but he didn't call for the
light to fulfill itself and it lurked impotently overhead.
He rose and sought his clothing, and the light followed
him darkly across the room.

He dressed, and not badly considering that he
dressed himself and that he dressed in the dark. In
younger days he had attended a school that thought
there was a relationship between character and an ability to dress in the dark. Villiers had abandoned the
practice for many years with obvious sad result. His

moral instructors would no doubt consider his present return to past habit a hopeful sign. He did not take the trouble to complete his robe with the garnish of a drapeau, however, which might have caused them to dwell and mull a bit.

He took up his cloak in the dark, but then was unable to locate his package. He patted and pawed and mumble-fingered the floor in the darkness, but though the feel of the carpeting was pleasant, he did not find the book. In irritation with himself, and feeling quite rightly that he was making a capitulation, Villiers at last called on the light.

It was slow to come up and only cast small shadows. It wasn't half the light it had been at dinnertime. Villiers looked up reproachfully and with seeming politeness it moved behind the crane of his neck. There it intensified a little, keeping its private glare fixed on the back of his head.

When Villiers lowered his gaze, it centered itself again directly above him. Even with the grace of reluctant illumination, he did not find the book immediately.

Sight confirmed that it was not on the table on which he believed he had left it. It was not where he had been searching on the floor close by the table. It was not anywhere in ready view.

Only then, prompted by the lingering impression of conducting a nighttime class in Evasion—a subject he in fact had never formally taught—did he begin to lift cushions. He found the book under the second cushion.

He nodded and eyed himself with proper suspicion in the wall mirror. Then he laughed.

He dusted himself, tugged and shrugged, and then put the package under his arm. The light centered itself properly and he had one last look in the glass. Then he proceeded into the hall.

The earlier sounds of moving and cleaning and decorating had largely been replaced by faint warm simmering smells of pudding and holiday, though Villiers did catch a distant trial blast of convivial music. The sound died.

The house was dark and only robots and mechanicals were afoot. They were busy. They had things to do. Purpose. The hour of Lord Semichastny's masquerade was not far distant, and since this year they had been allowed an opportunity for display usually denied by Lord Semichastny's sense of economy, they were determined to do more than they possibly could in the short time remaining.

Charles, faint yellow courtesy light shining, was waiting for Villiers when he reached the foot of the stairs.

"Good evening, sir," he said.

"Good evening," said Villiers.

Charles handed Villiers a letter. "Lord Semichastny instructed me to give this to you when you arose."

"Did the Duden mailboat arrive?"

"I'm sorry, sir. I don't know. Lord Semichastny said to tell you that he discovered this in reconsideration of his desk, and apologizes for the oversight, pleading a full stomach and the lateness of the hour. He promises to look yet again when he wakes."

"My uncle overelaborates his points," said Villiers. "Thank you, Charles."

The letter bore Villiers' personal address symbol as a sign that it was not a common bill or solicitation or an anonymously addressed bit of random trash. It had been opened before it came into Villiers' hands.

It was from Villiers' mother and it began, "I disap-
prove . . ." which was not at all her usual way. It
turned out, however, that what she disapproved of was
Villiers' association with her brother. The final para-
graphs were even addressed directly to Geoffrey on
the assumption that his habits hadn't altered, as indeed
they hadn't.

While Villiers was reading the letter, his light suddenly brightened appreciably. He looked up to see
Harbourne Firnhaber trotting down the stairs.

"You're up early," said Harbourne.

"I have immediate business in town," said Villiers,
holding up the packaged book by way of misdirection.

"Would you like me to mail that for you, sir?" asked
Charles.

"I think not," said Villiers. "And why are you up so
soon, Cousin?"

Harbourne said, "I'm to find masquerade guests for
Uncle's party. I thought to make an early start on it."

"Whom are you inviting?"

"Anyone, Milord Charteris. I shall sweep the streets
of town."

"You may not find many on the streets. Xochitl
Sodality of the Delbalso Monist Association is playing
Wonders and Marvels tonight and most people are
keeping to their homes. I saw few on my way here
tonight."

"But it was late then. It's earlier than that now,"
said Harbourne.

"True," said Villiers, "but I think it makes small
difference. They seemed bent on making a full night of
it. Be careful lest they take you for a Wonder and keep
you."

"Do you think they might take me for a Wonder?"

"It's perfectly possible. I fell into their hands myself."

"But apparently they didn't keep you."

"No," said Villiers. "They found me insufficiently marvelous and cast me back into the streets again to grow to larger size. Alas, I fear I have attained a final and insufficient height, and shall ultimately disappoint them."

In fact, Villiers had not been that disappointing. Small, yes, and no Ian Steele, but not without presence when he cared to make the point. As it had happened, Villiers had encountered the friend of a friend, and of course there had been no question about his movements once that had been established.

"Will you gentlemen have breakfast?" asked Charles.

In this world there are a million windows through which to see. There are a million mirrors, and a million prospects. The ordinary man accepts this, and if the world looks a little different to him one day and the next, or if his mirror shows him something new, it neither troubles nor surprises him. The variety lends roundness to life.

However, for those few raised to a single narrow squint the discovery of even a second perspective on the smoke and swirl of the evanescent world can be important, shocking and joyful. This is good if it leads to new vistas, and bad if the second perspective is mistaken for Final Truth.

Timur i Leng, vizier of Chagatay under Suyurghatmish, discovered one day that the world looks different from forty feet in the air and was overwhelmed. He gathered his army and overran Khorasan, Jurjan, Mazandaran, Sijistan, Azerbaijan, and Fars. In each place he raised a pyramid of skulls forty feet high and limped to the top in the hopes of recapturing that first thrilling rush—and missed the point completely.

Sir Henry the Trog stood in danger of similarly refining too greatly on a single new view of the world. He would not come out of his costume no matter what his wife said. He was quiet about it—when he did not forget himself and dance or sing to savor once again the puzzling and pleasing strangeness of it all—but he was adamant. He would not come out.

His mind had been busy and kept him from sleep, but at last he had fallen into warm electric dreams. When he woke he turned his woolly head and saw that his wife had risen. He did not seek her company immediately but lay awake and let the butterflies in his mind take spotted wing. He hummed.

He was still humming when he located Lady Oliphaunt eating a solitary breakfast. By the debris before her, she was nearly finished.

"Ah, my dear," he said. "Charles said I should find you here." And mused off into a hum again.

"No," she said, looking at him and then looking back at her buttered bun. "I'm not here." Meaning that she wished she weren't.

"I don't understand you," he said, not wishing to.

She said, "Henry—darling—won't you at least take the costume off for breakfast?"

She began to scour her plate with the last of her bun. To a lesser degree, she shared her husband's failing. When she was young she would never have dared to do anything so vulgar as mop her plate. It was only eventually that she had learned that anything is proper if it is done with supreme confidence and ultimate style, and now she scoured her plate when and as she pleased, carelessly, thoughtlessly, freely. If she had been sensitive to her own easy excess she might have been more easily forgiving of Sir Henry's.

He said, "Oh, thank you, but it isn't necessary. In fact I think it's a very good thing. It will give me practice in managing food. I shouldn't want to appear clumsy before the good people of Delbalso. We want to give them every reason to think well of Empire, and we must remember that ultimately it is we who will stand for Empire out here. Charles will be serving me here at any moment, I should think."

He began to experiment with Trog-handed shadow pictures with the aid of his light cone.

Lady Oliphaunt said, "I'm sorry, but I won't be able to stay and keep you company. The sooner I go to town the better. I have still to find a costume."

"That's true. That's true. But I dislike the thought of your traveling alone in the dark. Why don't you see whether Lord Charteris or Mr. Firnhaber will bear you company?"

"Charles said that both milord's nephews rose early and left in company for town. I've missed the opportunity, it seems, but I truly don't mind going alone. Truly not."

He gave that a moment's consideration. Then he said, "I'll bypass breakfast! I'll escort you to town myself. The least I can do is see that we complement each other."

Lady Oliphaunt was sadly lacking in apparent enthusiasm for this show of consideration. Perhaps she should never have married. The heart of marriage is a sharing of company and aim.

Instead she asked, "And would you be wearing that costume?"

"Well, yes, my dear. I thought . . ."

She turned her head to the wall and said definitely, "I won't go."

Lord Semichastny sat up in bed when Charles entered to serve him his breakfast melon. He had slept later than he intended, and he had contingencies on his mind. The melon was to provide him strength to cope.

Charles rolled to the bed and served breakfast. Besides melon, there was a toasted scone, sweetmold from Protopapis, an advance piece of crisply roasted skin and fat sliced from a goose in the kitchens, dogbone, drennel, and tea. However, Lord Semichastny had the courage of his compulsions and counted this mere dressing to the melon.

"Have there been any calls?" he asked before taking his first bite.

"None, milord. It has been generally quiet."

"None?"

"None, milord."

After a moment's reflection, Lord Semichastny began his breakfast. He needed at least the scone as fuel for his temper, so he dug in heartily the sooner to start the steam rising.

"I have another letter for Lord Charteris," he said. "Did you give him the first?"

"Yes, milord, but Lord Charteris has departed the house. He and Mr. Firnhaber left for town hours ago."

"Did he pick out a costume?"

"No, milord. I did suggest it to him as you said to do—most politely—but he said his attendance remained to be seen."

"He did, did he?"

"And he said that you overelaborate your points, milord."

"He did, did he?" Lord Semichastny looked at his robot butler as though suspecting him of taking delight in the simple messages he was entrusted to relay. Limited Volition hardly extends so far as delight.

"Your pardon, milord. May I be excused? I should be overseeing the musical arrangements."

"No, damn it! You'll stay until I give you leave to go. You say that Lord Charteris and Mr. Firnhaber left for town together?"

"Yes, milord."

"Well, perhaps Lord Charteris intends to lend a hand in locating a cross section of Delbalso for the fete."

"I think not, milord. He spoke of mailing a package and other business."

"Catlap!" said Lord Semichastny through his breakfast. "Catlap! Get out of here, Charles! Go answer the door. Go see to the music. Go."

However, some fifteen minutes later Lord Semichastny, chewing his piece of goose skin, wandered through the darkened house until he found Charles, who indeed was overseeing the musical arrangements. Within the limited sphere of running this house, Charles was a versatile creature, although in the wild world outside he would have been nearly helpless.

"Where are Sir Henry and Lady Oliphaunt?" Lord Semichastny asked. "I can't seem to find them."

"Gone to town, milord. They too," Charles

answered. "Would you like to review the music I've chosen?"

"As long as you know the tunes are those I like, I'm sure you will choose adequately. Did they travel with Lord Charteris and Mr. Firnhaber?"

"No, milord. They said something of choosing a costume for Lady Oliphaunt. Now I took it upon myself to suggest to Lady Oliphaunt that we could do very well for her here. Semiramis Among the Doves could be both popular and successful."

"What were you thinking of?" Lord Semichastny asked. "That's not for Amita. Semiramis Among the Doves is Kitty-Belle Armbruster's style."

"Oh, I'm sorry, sir. My taste is not good. Lady Oliphaunt had the good sense to share your opinion, milord, and rejected the suggestion. After some discussion, she and Sir Henry left in a flitter for town."

"And no one has called?"

"No, milord."

"But it's getting late!"

"Have no fear, milord. All shall be ready here before the hour. I think you will have reason to be proud of your loyal staff of robots and mechanicals."

But Lord Semichastny was not mollified. He paced through the empty house mumbling to himself. He took hasty notice of food, drink, music and decoration, but he did not pause for long. He waited for someone to come. He waited for someone to call. No one called. No one came. And so he paced.

At last he said, "I'm going into town. Run out a flitter, Charles."

And at first Charles was too busy to notice. Supervision is necessary if you expect a staff to do more than it possibly can. But Charles was not the only member of the Merry Major-Domos on Delbalso by happenstance. He was a member because he was capable of prodigies. His staff not only did more than it possibly could, but it finished with time to spare.

It was only then that Charles truly noticed that the house was empty. All the humans had gone away.

Charles had done exactly as he ought, and the party was ready. But there were no people.

The house was without light. Even Charles' yellow courtesy light no longer glowed. It was not needed.

With all ready for service—food held hot and cold in stasis, walls strung, entertainments ready for release on command or trip, mechanicals shiny and well-rehearsed, and flower petals in an urn by the door—there was no one to serve.

Charles rolled to the dressing room, and there he looked for some time at a green polkadotted silk sarong, a diaphanous blouse of cream, and an orange tarboosh. It was only at times like this that being a chattel weighed heavily. He had been built to serve, after all. But not to be abused by orange! At last, however, thinking that he heard the approach of a flitter, he put the uniform on. And he was right— orange did not become him.

He was wrong, however, in thinking he detected a flitter. When he returned upstairs, he found nothing but the robots and mechanicals of the house in gathering. He shooed them into the main hall to wait.

They waited and they wondered.

"Will the people come?" they asked.

"Who knows?" Charles said. "Be patient."

To pass the time, he told them stories in the dark hall as he often had on winter nights when the house was closed and the robots wondered about spring and the reality of Lord Semichastny.

He began, "There was a man dwelt by a church-yard," which is a good story, full of sprites and gob-lins, though a trifle sad. However, the mechanicals had hard it too often before and cried him halt.

"Tell another story," they said.

"And let it be scary," said the shiny serving table that had brought the message to Villiers.

"But not too scary," they said.

So Charles began again:

"Once there was an old man and a woman and a little household robot, and they all lived in a house made of hempstalks. The old man had a dog, and he was a little dog, and the little dog's name was Turpie. And one night the Hobyahs came and said, 'Hobyah! Hobyah! Hobyah! Tear down the hempstalks. Eat up the old man. Eat up the old woman. Carry off the little house-hold robot!' But little dog Turpie barked so that the Hobyahs ran off."

And he held the attention of the room. As they waited.

7

IF MY mother's advice were taken as widely as she would give it, every man would have two professions. For the common man in a common time, two professions do keep life from becoming commonplace, or so my mother would have it. In headier times, when the palm flourishes and the dates hang heavy and sweet, a second interest keeps a man from bruiting the price of dates over his second helping of date-nut pudding and being a bore to his guests. And in times of drouth, a second skill keeps a man.

Like much of the folk wisdom inherited from her simple peasant ancestors, this is sensible conservative advice. It keeps men alive and peasants peasants.

Every man should have two professions—at the least—for reasons of security. But lest security become cloying, one of the professions should be a flyer. Something like poetry, or astrology. Or selling ornamental rugs.

Poetry and astrology each had a brief moment of glory, poetry in the days when language was wild and whirling and a man with his words about him could kill with a lightning phrase, and astrology when it was finally realized that everything in the universe affects everything else and that something as consequential as a star or planet must have its effects on human lives. But poetry became shackled by grammars and dictionaries, and astrology became lost in the science of universal ecology. Astrology and poetry have been secondary professions ever since, limited by the normal modesty of people who do not care to have their names linked with stars unless it be done surpassingly well.

As for ornamental rugs, they are notoriously uncertain.

And it is true that two ordinarily chancy professions can be strangely successful in combination. Any pairing of poetry, astrology and ornamental rugs, for instance, can mean synergetic miracles.

And the trinity, the three-in-one, can mean a saint, a ruler of the sevagram, or Omar Khayyám. Unfortunately, the combination is rare.

A great heavy bell rolled and tolled above them as Slyne and McBe harried the midnight streets. They coursed a long, sloping cobbleway. Slyne felt close to the questionable Trog. McBe felt terror held in abeyance. As long as he concentrated on following Slyne and didn't think, he was functional, but when they paused or when he thought, he was afraid.

As the last bell peal finished echoing, they were suddenly surrounded by a crowd of middle-aged men in yellow shorts with embroidered jumper fronts.

"Hold," they said.

Slyne held, feeling the game whose dim track he had followed so well would escape him. When Slyne stopped, McBe stopped, too. It was that, and not the cry to hold, that caused him to look up. When he saw the strange yellow circle, he nearly fell. He kept his feet by seizing Slyne's moleskin arm.

"Oh, not now," said Slyne in a mixed agony of exaltation and exasperation. He inhaled once, a quick sniff, and then he said, "Who are you?"

One swept off a feathered cockade in a grandiose gesture, limited by fat. "Rafael Abdelnoor of the Xochitl Sodality, at your service. You can tell by our colors, of course, that we belong to Schermerhorn House, the best house in the best Monist Association in the quadrant."

Another said reprovingly, "Don't be un-Monist, Rafe."

"Sorry," said the first, chastened. In less inflated tones, he said, "We're playing Wonders and Marvels tonight. And we've chosen you."

Then he said to his critic, "I was just enjoying myself."

Slyne said, "I am sorry. It cannot be. We—my assistant and I—are on urgent affairs on behalf of the Empire. Much as we would like to observe your rituals, I am afraid that we cannot stay."

Abdelnoor said, "But you're *here*. That means you're playing. You shouldn't be out tonight if you're not serious about playing. By the way, what are you?"

To this pertinent question, Slyne replied, "I am an Auxiliary Executive Overseer (NIS/9) (Pending)."

This was apparent to the trained eye from his uniform, right down to the (Pending), but Slyne did not expect a trained eye in this crowd, so he included the fact.

"No. No, no. What *are* you? What is your ethnos?"

"Oh. I am an Orthodoxou."

"Well, we haven't had one of those before."

What happened next is unpleasant to recount. Mr. Abdelnoor of the Xochitl Sodality had one set of plans for the night and Mr. Slyne of the Rock had another. If they had reasoned calmly with each other, no doubt they could have come to agreement—perhaps a third alternative altogether halfway between the mountains and the seashore. However, they lost their tempers, raised their voices and fell into rhetoric.

When the subject became the relative power to command of the Nashuite Empire and the Schermerhorn Chapter of the Xochitl Sodality, windows were opened and the people of the neighborhood made comment.

"Take it away from here! We let you have the streets. Leave us a little peace."

Mr. Abdelnoor settled his point, which was that while the power of the Nashuite Empire was concededly great, so was it also distant, and that the power of the Schermerhorn Chapter of the Xochitl Sodality, overall totaling considerably less, was immediately somewhat the greater, by having Mr. Slyne picked up bodily by two mature initiates and carried off through the streets. They didn't pick up Mr. McBe and carry him off, perhaps out of oversight. After all, when it is dark and noisy and sudden, it is extremely easy to be careless of details.

McBe ran after them protesting the oversight, but they were laughing and took no notice. He overtook a trailing two.

"Wait, there! What are you doing with Mr. Slyne?"

"Ho-ho," they said.

The two turned upon him and used him hardly. They whipped a blindfold over his eyes, and laughed, and spun him dizzyingly until he sat down plump on the damp cobbles.

And then they ran off, their middle-aged feet thumping away into the universal dark that surrounded McBe's unsettled mind and blindfolded eyes. He sat on the street and cried, and very slowly took the blindfold off. He unknotted it and smoothed it, and then folded it neatly.

While he sat, folding and crying and wondering desolately what to do, happy Christian bells of joy began to chime again.

It was near peelgrunt, and Villiers had not yet arrived. Parini was not only awake, but agitated.

"Where is he?" he asked. "Do you suppose he took me overseriously when I told him to let us have a good sleep? I never considered him to have much of a sense of humor."

Miriam Parini said, "But of what use? Those papers for that beast haven't come."

"True, but the name has. And Villiers will pay twenty royals for that. What could Treleaven have been thinking of to change his mind so suddenly? Old men are too capricious."

He began to pace. With Treleaven's departure, he was suddenly dependent on Villiers' purse to pay his way free of the Winter-Summer Laws. He tried to see where the advantage lay, and the arguments that would emphasize the advantage. His biggest argument was that he had the name of the man who had twice hired the notorious assassin, Solomon "Biff" Dreznik, to put a period to Villiers' life. That was substantial information.

"Jules, could we ask Zvegintzov's man for money away? Once off Delbalso we could pay them back in no time, and they know that."

He stopped. "Not after I just pressured the name out of them. Besides, Zvegintzov's man was leaving when he called me. There's no one left to borrow from."

"What are we going to do?"

"Wait for Villiers," Parini said. "I suppose I could call around and see what I can find out. Perhaps somebody knows something."

"Perhaps somebody can tell what happened to the mail from Duden," his wife said.

"I'll ask," he said.

He hurried off to his communications network, cutting through the patio. The Christian's bells were ringing again and he wondered whether the Christian got the same pleasure from his bells that he got from his communications network. As it happened, the Christian did.

Slyne was not carried far. He would not cooperate with his yellow-suited captors of Schermerhorn House. He writhed. He kicked. When set down, he would not stand. When picked up again, he was not soothed. He seemed upset. And throughout he made steady complaint. It was not easy to suppress his remarks since they issued from behind the mesh of his sensory amplifier. One hand tried and was nipped severely.

Slyne's dander was up:

"Dare manhandle an (NIS/9) (Pending)! They have their eye on me, and you will be held to strict accounting for this. They wouldn't have solved the Diced Strawberry Affair without me!"

That is the trouble with those who love their organizations too dearly. In time of trouble they rely on them, and personal initiative is lost. Slyne was not alone in this. His captors were no better.

Slyne was an uncompromising poor sport, and those carrying him soon grew weary.

"He just won't play," they said to Abdelnoor.

After Abdelnoor had his own turn at carrying Slyne—and it would have been un-Monist for him not to have had a turn—he was forced to agree. So he made a signal and they set Slyne down on the pavement.

Abdelnoor faced Slyne severely. He wagged his finger at the wet tip of Slyne's nose.

"I've never met one of your kind before—an Orthodoxou. But I'll remember you and I'll see that the word gets passed along. I've never seen such behavior. I suppose it's only what can be expected from the Rock. I can tell you one thing, you'll never have another chance to play. If you can't play properly, we just don't want you around!"

And the body of men all turned away from Slyne and showed him their backs all the way around the corner.

Slyne cocked his head and sampled the night through his amplifier. There was the overwhelming sound of bells.

He thought of tracking back to find the Trog's trail, and then the image of a despairing McBe came to him. He inhaled reflexively.

"Is it peelgrunt yet?" Villiers asked when he was brought his meal by Ozu Xenakis.

Xenakis ran a bistro and had the greens concession in Delbalso. He charged small fees for use of the green and gardens by singles, couples and parties, and his bistro profits paid for the rest. His windows overlooked the green, making his place an easy one for custom to retire to in bad weather, and in good weather the view was pleasant. Even now, in artifical light, it was live and inviting. In addition, as the only spot on Delbalso with an off-world flavor—for Xenakis had spent the first twenty-four years of his life on Luvashe and Posada—his *Centre* was a popular spot for travelers and transients, and the only place on Delbalso mentioned by Wu and Fabricant. It was the place that Lady Oliphaunt had set for her appointment with Villiers— the only place in town fit for an appointment.

Xenakis himself was a good-natured man with over-large teeth and a ready willingness to talk with anyone on his own subject. He sometimes wondered if the teeth were bad for business and considered having them altered.

"Oh, it's not yet peelgrunt," he said. "When it is, you'll know, right enough. This is the best spot in Delbalso, on Delbalso, for peelgrunt."

While Villiers was eating, content for the moment with his book posted and peelgrunt still ahead, two men entered the bistro. It was obvious from their manner that they were no more from Delbalso than Xenakis or

Villiers. They sat down and ordered. They seemed at odds with the world, finding it duller than they liked.

They were Civilian Research Specialists imported to Delbalso by the Imperial Government to make subtle star sightings and assessments on behalf of the Universal Pantograph Project. This great machine, when completed, it was hoped would model the universe with sufficient exactitude that anticipations might be made. Nashua's offices were filled with humble men anxious to use any tool that came to hand to further the Empire and Good, and already drooling in anticipation of the Universal Pantograph.

These two men were not power brokers, however. They merely did simple jobs and were paid for them, and the eventual results of their work were distant enough to lack immediacy for them.

One said, "Let's go back to the Castle." He looked around the room, empty but for Villiers and Xenakis. "Nothing at all is doing tonight."

"Let's look a little longer," the other said. "It will be weeks before we have another night."

"Where is everyone?" the first asked. "The only people we saw were some older men running around in red shorts."

"Oh, those would be from Montague House," said Xenakis. "It's the Monist Association—Xochitl Sodality tonight. Things tend to be quiet on a Sodality night, unless they let you play. Most people stay at home. As you can see, I'm working alone."

"Monists? Oh, Monists, yes. They're the ones who put over those Winter-Summer Laws, aren't they?" one of them said.

And the other said, "They asked us if we were

Wonders and Marvels. We said we were just plain us, and they told us to go back to the Rock.''

"They meant the Castle," said Xenakis. "It's just a way of speaking they have here.''

He said it gently. He didn't know what he thought until he said it, and what he said depended in major on who his trade was. A good diplomatic publican and a good man, by his lights.

And the first said to the second, ''I told you that you shouldn't have said we were just us. You should have dressed us up a bit. If you'd told them we were pantographers, maybe they wouldn't have sent us away.''

Xenakis said, "Well, maybe you can try again later. They'll be playing all night. The Monists aren't really so bad when you get to know them. They weren't really behind the Winter-Summer Laws. That was just a story that was given out. The truth is that the town wanted to get rid of Viscount Semichastny, who lives here in the summer and throws extreme parties. When he's gone, they'll change things back in a year or two.''

''Oh, yes,'' said the first pantographer. ''Lord Semichastny. I heard about him, too.''

"He sold me the sod for the greens out there,'' Xenakis said, pointing. ''I've talked to him several times. He's really not so bad, either. Not at heart.''

Harbourne Firnhaber came to the early conclusion that his noble new-found cousin was right in one regard. There were few people on the streets.

He had made the mistake of anticipating the town and the task, and neither proved to be what he had pictured. All too often we mistake our own habits, interests and ambitions for universal facts, not realizing that there are one or two families that do not sit down to Sunday dinner at three. Harbourne had thought that since there was nothing that he would have liked better in his planet-bound days than to be invited to a viscount's party, he would have no trouble in filling Lord Semichastny's maison with louts and gawkers. But just as Lord Charteris had said, the night and streets were empty.

Harbourne had left his cousin in an empty bistro and begun to walk. And he saw no one, not even the Xochitl Sodality of whom Charteris had warned him. As time passed, his anticipations curdled and he began to suspect that he had made a bad bargain.

He stopped in the street and looked about him. In the black heights he could hear bells. They sounded in better spirits than he and played a tune.

He looked at the houses about him and wondered whether he ought to start knocking at one door and the next. In the face of empty streets, it was the next step to take, but he wasn't prompt to take it. Lord Semichastny had been right. These were people the like of which he no longer knew and no longer cared to know.

He might be capable of knocking and asking if he had to. He rather thought he was. But he didn't relish the idea.

And then he saw a man ahead of him on the street. It was a man of a dignified age wearing a white mantle with a blue fringe.

Harbourne almost broke into a run, but managed to control himself. He walked toward the man and when they came together he said, "Good even, sir."

At least the man was clean.

"Good evening," the man said with manners, if not manner. It was Ossian Chimmeroon.

Harbourne presented his proposition. He found that once begun, the words were not difficult.

He introduced himself and extended an invitation to a party on behalf of Lord Geoffrey Semichastny. As he put it, it sounded like splendid fun.

"Lord Semichastny feels that he has neglected his Delbalso neighbors and desires this chance to entertain them, as well as give them the opportunity of meeting Sir Henry Oliphaunt, the new Empire Administrator."

Chimmeroon said, "Not in these clothes."

"Lord Semichastny wishes to present the informal atmosphere of Delbalso—the better to put Sir Henry at ease. He said 'come-as-you-are.' "

"Oh, no," said Chimmeroon. "I just threw this on when we set out to look for Badrian Beaufils. Are you sure you mean Lord Semichastny?"

"Oh, yes. Yes."

"And the Empire Administrator?"

"In company with his lady."

"And a party."

"It's all true," said Harbourne. "Isn't it just like a dream?"

"Yes. It's been a long night. But I can't go," Chimmeroon said definitely. "I still must find Badrian Beaufils. Tell me, Friend Harcourt . . ."

"Harbourne."

"Have you seen a group of men of an age somewhat younger than mine, all dressed in blue, and some with hats and feathers?"

"No," said Harbourne. "Have you seen anyone at all?"

Between the dark and the daylight on the planet of Delbalso, when the night is beginning to bore, there comes a pause in the night's occupations when solitary peels, ordinarily content to cling torpidly to their tree branches, carefully unwrap themselves and slide to the ground for a convivial stretch. The signal for movement is a heavy grunt from the least peel, a complaint of muscles too long cramped, answered by a chorus of confirming grunts from the neighboring branches, and then echoed in all the trees surrounding. The air is filled with common complaint and common decision. The break is brief, and when their stretch is done, the peels wind their way back to a new branch and a symbiotic slumber that lasts until dawn.

Villiers left the *Centre* at peelgrunt. The peels in the park around the town green were honored, admired and pampered, and in the green itself they were presented with a beautiful spot to foregather. In return, they were expected to grunt lustily, which I am pleased to say they did.

Xenakis said, "There's your peelgrunt. From the sound I'd say it will be good weather tonight, clear until morning. If you'll go to the windows, in a minute or two you will see the peels beginning to foregather."

"Thank you," said Villiers, rising, "but I must be on my way. I'll catch a look from the street."

"It's not the same," said Xenakis. "Not the same at all. We have the best view of the green right here. The Xochitl Sodality will be playing Wonders and Marvels there later tonight. Most local people—those that aren't Monists—tend to see it as common, but I enjoy watching it. I recommend it to you.''

"I may take your recommendation,'' said Villiers. "Indeed I had some notion of a look at the Xochitl Sodality.''

As Villiers left, Xenakis and the pantographers were standing at the window and chuckling down at the gathering peels. Villiers took the front steps down to the cobble street and then turned right. He did take his promised look at the peels. However, Xenakis had been right. The view was inferior. Bits and pieces only of the green could be seen through the deliberate distractions of the trees, and of the peels Villiers could have said little but that they were like black and brown wriggling fur boas. Villiers did not pause with his look, but set off up the hill toward Parini's, condemned to business in others' playtime.

The street climbed the hill in steps. Villiers was on the second flight when he heard one of his names called. It was "Lord Charteris"—and while that choice of name did not announce the caller, it did limit him to the lesser part of Villiers' acquaintance.

He turned. "Ah, Mr. Slyne. It is a pleasant evening for exercise.''

Slyne hurried up. He said, "These people just don't have any idea of proper respect for the Empire. I intend to speak to the new Administrator. Have you seen my assistant, Mr. McBe? They took me away from him. He was the young man who questioned your papers. Oh, I'm so agitated.''

He removed his sensory amplifier to calm himself.

Sensory amplifiers are useful, particularly to Orthodoxous, but they are a doubtful thing for an upset mind.

"I remember him," said Villiers. ."However, I haven't seen him since I left Castle Rock."

"Oh, I'm worried," said Slyne. "We were separated by circumstance and now he is alone in the night. Did you hear that series of roars?"

"Peelgrunt, perhaps?"

Slyne considered what his roars might have been without benefit of the night, his state of mind and his amplifier.

"They might have been grunts. But it must have unnerved him. He lacks confidence. I noted that tonight and I was attempting to strengthen his resolve. You must remember. You saw me."

"I do remember," said Villiers.

On the heights of Castle Rock another ship landed. From where they stood, the green was not visible, but its lights were. There were lights in scatterings through the town and then the great solid massif standing above the opposite slope, big and black and lit by lightning, soundless lightning. Soundless ship. No growl of energy. The ship descended in silent display and the only sound that Villiers could hear was the sound of Christian bells.

Slyne fitted his amplifier over his head the better to consider the ship. He still could not hear it, though his view of it was substantially improved. However, the bells were amplified sufficiently to cause him extreme agitation, so he removed the amplifier again.

"I keep having to take it off," he said. "I'm so

disturbed. I can't concentrate. Why does the ship make no sound? Why do the bells ring?''

Villiers said, ''I believe the neighborhood has acoustical advantages which are reflected in the rents. The bells ring in Christian celebration.''

''It's strange. It's strange,'' said Slyne. ''I've never been in a place like this before. What can't happen to me?''

He meant to say ''McBe'' but he said ''me.'' It shocked him, because he considered himself safe and stable and in control. It was his fortune that he had never been on Livermore, far more disconcerting than Delbalso.

He took himself in hand to hear Villiers say, ''Perhaps being separated from you will be the very making of him, sir. He may discover that he has resources.''

''Oh, he's not ready,'' said Slyne. ''I only realize it now. We were close behind that Trog, ready to take him in hand and properly examine his papers. You remember the Trog.''

''I do remember.''

''You haven't seen him again, have you?''

''No,'' said Villiers. ''Not since I departed Castle Rock.''

''We were very close to the Trog when another ship landed. Then it was bells. Then we fell into the hands of Monists. Them,'' he said bleakly.

And he was right. They were in the process of being surrounded by a band in yellow. Monists, to be sure. And Schermerhorn House. And . . .

''Rafael Abdelnoor, at your service.'' Abdelnoor

swept off his hat. Only then did he recognize Slyne and he sighed and turned to Villiers and put his hat back on.

"I'm not playing," said Slyne.

"I know that you are not," said Abdelnoor. "Sir, are you?"

"Of course," said Villiers.

"Then I should inform you that you have been chosen our official Marvel for the night. Please come along."

"You wish me to be your Marvel? I'm sure you must be able to do better."

"True," said Abdelnoor. "But it's growing late. Sometimes we must make do."

8

THE AMOEBA only knows as much of the universe as it can touch, and its direct image of the world is necessarily incomplete. But generation to generation the amoeba remembers what it has touched, and builds and builds its picture.

We know at first hand a bountiful universe beyond the amoeba's dreams. We are the amoeba's dreams, the result of its striving to know more of the universe. And generation to generation, we remember what we have touched, and build and build our picture.

When man first started counting, he thought he had five senses: hearing, sight, taste, smell and touch. On a recount he discovered that subsumed under touch were at least three senses, separate and distinct—pressure, temperature, and texture—and that subsumed under taste were at least two.

He kept counting, and added the vestibular and kinesthetic senses. And the so-called Synesthetic Gearbox, which added confusion to sense.

One count totaled twenty-six, and another thirty-two. The definitive study by DeJudicibus in 1107 listed seventeen common human senses, from sight and smell to esthetics and self-awareness, and twenty more senses as rare, indistinct or only rumored.

The seventeen basic senses appear in every combination and degree in humans, the variance accounting for so many of our everyday differences in opinion. Any one sense may be strengthened to impressive limits by attention, experience and practice. But even all seventeen senses at their limit yield an imperfect picture of the universe. Subtle harmonies lie beyond our detection. The stars sing songs no man has ever heard.

However, if man doesn't hear the songs the stars sing, there are those that do. The Bessain, for instance, have been engaged in an eon-long conversation with their star to claimed mutual benefit.

And we have our strengths. Our senses are more than receptors. They acknowledge the presence of other sensitive concentrations of energy. Without sight—and our appreciation—the stars would not shine.

The Bessain report their star is delighted that its theoretical efforts are appreciated. So ask not for whom the stars shine. They shine for thee, and they are glad to do it.

Harbourne Firnhaber was a convinced Realist. He believed so strongly that words were things that he expected to feel significantly different and better on that day on which he somehow fulfilled his ambition and came into possession of a title. And it was as a

Realist, cowed by the size and shape of the word "Monist," that he stood outside Joralemon House nerving himself to knock. It was the single-minded unity of the word that he believed and feared. He felt dwarfed by it.

After a time, however, his ambitions got the better of his disquiet, and he tested the door. He sounded it twice, with every evidence of firm conviction.

The door was opened by a warder in the blue of Joralemon. It matched the flag over the door and the purfling on Ossian Chimmeroon's gaberdine.

"Good evening, sir," the warder said. "How may I help you?"

"I bear an invitation from Lord Semichastny," said Harbourne, and made his explanations. He spoke plausibly and winningly. "And he wishes the entire . . . household here to make the most of his hospitality."

"Why, that's very generous," said the warder. "Come right in. Did you say Lord Semichastny?"

"Yes, indeed," said Harbourne.

"Lord Semichastny. Well, well. I never thought of him as a generous man."

"Oh, he's a very generous man. He is known widely for his generosity to orphans. And he has treated me as though I were a member of his own family. I'm confident that you'll have a good time."

With the door closed behind Harbourne, the warder said, "I'll have your invitation put to the House. I almost wish I didn't have the honor of duty. I'd like to go myself."

Harbourne was pleased by the warder's friendliness. He could feel the tension leaving his tightly bound stomach muscles.

"By all means, find a substitute and come," Harbourne said.

"I'll only be a few minutes," the warder said. He showed Harbourne to a chair and handed him several brochures describing both the Monists and their philosophy and the special attractions of membership in Joralemon House. "You might read these to while the time."

Harbourne did thumb the brochures, but found the illustrations unexciting and the textual argument uncompelling. He studied the parquetry floor until the warder returned. Then he stood.

"Yes," he said.

The warder was apologetic. "I just came on duty," he said. "I'm sorry to say that it escaped my notice, but tonight as it happens is Xochitl Sodality. It's their night. No one else feels much like going out."

"You asked them?"

"Oh, yes. I asked anyway and everyone said they didn't think so. I was told to say thank you on behalf of everyone. Do keep us in mind for another time."

"I understand," said Harbourne, who did not understand.

"By the way," said the warder. "What did you think of the brochures? The literature I gave you?"

Harbourne looked down at the brochures he still held in his left hand.

"Very interesting," he said. And under the warder's eye he put the brochures in his coat. He felt he had to do it.

It was around the hub of the night in the streets of Delbalso when a consolidated party of the Greens of

118

Pierrepont, agreed on their Trog Marvel, met a much smaller party of the Blues of Joralemon, with no Marvel or Wonder at all. It was a party of three led by young—for the Xochitl Sodality—Badrian Beaufils, the same party from Joralemon encountered by Villiers earlier in the night.

And the Greens called out, "Aha," and made a point of showing their Wonder. They didn't care. They felt secure.

And the Blues hung their heads, because they did care and they had no Marvel and the night was passing.

Standing amidst the original quartet who had co-opted him, and further surrounded by succeeding additions of Pierrepont Sodality members, Torve's view of the world had been limited. But when the Joralemon Blues were encountered, the surrounding herd split wide to display Torve. And in that moment he saw Badrian Beaufils and recognized him.

And in that moment, Badrian Beaufils lifted his hung head to view the Greens' Marvel. And he recognized the pen pal whom Villiers had spoken of earlier in the night. Torve the Trog was not only on Delbalso, he was *here*.

They bounded toward each other to the sweet accompaniment of hearty happy Christian bells and huzzahs from some in both Green and Blue, and they embraced.

"Hey," cried Cohen, Newman, Zimmerman and Rose. "That's *our* Marvel!" And they believed he was.

When Badrian Beaufils understood, he was not happy. "Well, if Ossian Chimmeroon was bringing him to me, I don't think you ought to have him. He's my pen pal, after all.''

"Ah, but we saw him first as a Marvel," said the four. "And Ossian Chimmeroon is no longer in the Xochitl Sodality."

"What is problem?" Torve inquired of his friend. "World has many Wonders." In the afterglow of bells he said, "There is Christian. Why not him?"

"A Christian?" said Badrian Beaufils. "What is marvelous about that?"

But one of his fellows said, "It's not a bad suggestion, Badrian. The hour is growing late and for our presumption in setting out as only three we ought to return with something."

"All right," said Beaufils.

"We'll watch," said one of the Greens.

"Yes," said Rose, feeling expansive with the issue won. "We'll give you encouragement."

They traveled in a large party up the streets to the Christian's house. It was fronted by the blank face of his bell tower. There was an arched gate and a court within, but the gate was closed.

"Christians," said Beaufils, looking at the closed gate. "They're too exclusive. You notice there isn't even a bell to signal the house."

They milled about the street in front of the gate. Even if there had been a way to signal the house, it seemed that the Christian's attention was on his chimes. They were ringing again.

"Is holiday, I think," said Torve. He counted on his four fingers three times. "Yes, is Twelfthtide. Old Christian day of holly. See you?" He held up his four fingers three times. "Is twelve."

He called to his friends Zimmerman, Newman, Cohen and Rose: "Do you know Epiphany song, "Twelve Days of Christmas'?"

"No," they said. But they liked to sing in front of their fellows, so while the bells were ringing above them, Torve taught them the song—which, after all, has a simple tune and repetitive lyrics. They worked on their parts until the bells ceased and then they sang the song.

Torve's memory of the words was imperfect, but the principle was clear, and he was followed by Rose, Zimmerman, Newman and Cohen, and they by the rest of the Xochitl Sodality.

By the third "partridge in a pear tree" they had a visible witness in the bell tower. They persevered to the end of the song, however. And the man in the tower applauded.

Then Torve called up, "Hello. Is Wonders and Marvels night. Do you want to be a Marvel?"

"Me?" the man said. "You want me to be a Marvel? I never thought that would ever happen. Me a Marvel? How splendid. I'll be right down to let you in."

He came down and opened the gate. "Come in," he said and Torve and all the Blues and Greens entered the courtyard. He was a ruddy little man and he said his name was Dodd.

"And I'm Badrian Beaufils. You'll be our Wonder. We're with Joralemon House. These other men are from Pierrepont."

"My side is Joralemon?"

"That's right."

"Are you sure you mean me?"

"Oh, yes," said Badrian Beaufils, feeling that an

apology was owed. Then he offered, "I've always enjoyed your bells."

"You have?" said Dodd. "I wasn't sure that anyone listened. You really do?"

Several Sodality members, both Blues and Greens, assured him that they did. Dodd was delighted.

"Er, you are our first Christian," said Badrian Beaufils. "Can you tell us your points of strength so that we can offer the best possible presentation?"

"Oh, but I'm not a Christian," Dodd said.

"You're not?"

"Oh, no. Not really. I'm a Christian historian. I don't believe. I just keep track of things. Would you like to see my collection?"

They all agreed that they would, and Mr. Dodd took them inside. He apologized for the condition of things. The condition of things was largely piles. He got shipments of material all the time and never had it completely sorted.

He served them tea and biscuits while they looked. There were piles of surplices and wimples. There were candles and missals, collection plates, beads, lunules, censers, thuribles, aspergillums and ciboria. The Xochitl Sodality found it a whole new world.

Then he took them to see his personal display. This room was much neater. He had a ring that had belonged to Pope Leo VIII, whose pontificate was disputed. He had a comparative wall chart of tonsure patterns. He had a religious scroll containing an apocryphal Christian gospel with an authenticated history all the way back to the beginning of the Common Era, and sufficient age to place its origin at the beginning of the era preceding. He had a putative piece of the True Cross, also of the proper age, and with a thousand years more documentation than the scroll.

"Is fascinating," said Torve the Trog.

Before they were done viewing, Rose drew Badrian Beaufils aside and asked if he might not consider trading Wonders. He was thinking how effectively Dodd and his collection could be presented by a quartet singing "The Twelve Days of Christmas." He didn't even pause to consider from whom he had learned the song. Badrian Beaufils quite rightly turned him down out of loyalty to his friend Torve.

"I was expecting you at peelgrunt," said Jules Parini.

"I was unavoidably detained, sir," said Villiers. "I hope you weren't inconvenienced."

"Come in off the doorstep. We were at breakfast. Would you care to join us?"

"Thank you, no," said Villiers. "I've eaten. Have the papers arrived?"

Parini said, "No, I'm sorry. The mails haven't been delivered. I expect them at any moment. My sources tell me the delay may be due to some local Monist shenanigans. I was beginning to fear that you might have fallen into their hands."

"As in fact I did," said Villiers.

"Oh, that's terrible."

"Not really," said Villiers. "I have no objection to Monists. They have an extremely good idea, but they are too single-minded about it. I won free quite honestly by touting my captors onto two willing astrologers whom all agree are far more marvelous than I—and more interested in the game. I did promise to attend the judging, if I find it possible."

"Although I don't have your papers," said Parini, "I do have news for you. I have the name of your assassin's employer. Do you still have interest in it?"

"Yes, I do."

"What was the figure we were speaking of?"

"The figure we were speaking of was twenty royals. However, sir, I have to tell you that the money was not where I expected to find it."

"No?" Parini said suspiciously. He was not certain whether Villiers was bargaining with him, flighting him, or speaking honestly.

"No. I lack the price of your information—unless you would apply my credit with you toward this assassin's name. Are you sure the papers are on their way?"

"I am."

"Then that presents a problem," said Villiers. "I am a good deal less certain of ever coming together with my money."

"Are you bargaining?" Parini asked. "You should realize that there is small room for bargain."

"I recognize your price," said Villiers. "I simply cannot presently meet it. Do you have immediate need for money?"

Parini was embarrassed by the question. He enjoyed boasting of the tuition payments at Miss McBurney's as though they made small difference to his pocket. To admit of a need for money was painful, but still the prospect of a sojourn under the Winter-Summer Laws was even more painful to consider.

"Some small need," Parini said. "Can you give me a draft, perhaps?"

This showed his incipient desperation. He didn't usually speak of drafts to people who had dealt with him before and had some notion of what he did with drafts.

"I'm sorry, Mr. Parini," said Villiers. "My only asset is an empty and undeveloped planet I have by bequest and could not bear to part with. All the rest is prospects and largesse, and the largesse is beyond my reach. However, let me consider. Are you familiar with my uncle, Lord Semichastny?"

"Is he your uncle? I wasn't aware that you were quite that prominently connected, Mr. Villiers."

"Didn't Zvegintzov tell you that? Yes, Lord Semichastny is my uncle. He has scheduled to give a party tonight, which, because of the interference of the Winter-Summer Laws, I suspect will not take place. He has as much as said that my money will be produced if I attend his masque."

"I hadn't heard of it," said Parini. "My sources seem to have failed me."

"He has need of guests and does not care particularly who they might be. On his behalf, I invite you and Mrs. Parini to the masque. Make what profit you can of the invitation."

Parini's feelings were mixed. He had passed as the offspring of a marquis to enter his daughter at Miss McBurney's, but he preferred to operate at a lower and more comfortable level of society.

Villiers said, "As for me, I shall drum up the company for my uncle's party, since he seems determined to have one."

"And you will then pay me twenty royals for the name?"

Villiers said, "No. I have no great confidence in my uncle's 'as-much-as-saids.' I can guarantee you nothing. Merely, I want the name and you need money. If we are to have a party, let it be one we can both enjoy."

"Are you proposing partnership? Do I understand you?" said Parini.

"I'm suggesting mutual effort—you for your profit, I for mine."

"A speculative venture?"

"A speculative venture. And if you should visit Lord Semichastny's study to admire his ornamental rugs, you might have a look around for a draft to my name by the Duke of Tremont-Michaud."

"I believe I understand," said Parini.

They discussed the matter for some few more minutes and came to agreement. When Villiers had left, Parini returned to his breakfast.

The first thing he said to his wife was, "Villiers has changed. Five years ago he would have insisted on having the assassin's name."

"No money?" she said.

"No money," he said. "I'm still to give him the papers when they come. We are to meet at Lord Semichastny's country home. Where is Annie?"

Her place at the table was empty, the result of an altercation terminated by authority.

Mrs. Parini said, "I sent her to her room. She said *poggar* and *hobyah* and *beng*. I wish you would speak to her about it."

126

"I will," said her husband. "However, for now put on your best cherry-picking clothes. We are going to a party to raise money."

The stars rolled apple-down-dilly in their courses overhead, painting tracks of white-gold across enfolding blackness. The night breath was sweet and heart-pounding. Sir Henry the Trog hopped through the streets of the town, minddancing with crystal cocoons, heartsprung.

He felt himself to be a Trog. He believed himself to be a Trog. It was the most exciting thing that had ever happened to him. He didn't understand it, but he didn't want it to end.

He saw the world as he was sure a Trog must see it. Sharper. Clearer. In focus for the first time. It was a joy to run and hop and dance, to look and see things for the first time from a new angle. Close one eye. Close the other eye. Blink. Blink. And one world from two angles. Oh, so new, so rare.

The night was a frabjous treat.

Sir Henry the Trog, Sir Henry the Trog, *hallah, hallah, hallah*.

He had misplaced Lady Oliphaunt, but he hardly cared. Far more important, he had misplaced Sir Henry Oliphaunt and he was enjoying himself completely for perhaps the first time. Yes, yes, yes.

He exulted, caught in the grip of a major miracle.

But then his reverie was interrupted by someone thin and brown and dressed in Imperial Service uniform. The uniform of an Assistant.

It was Jerzy McBe, caught in the grip of his own

miracle. His miracle was that he was still functioning and doing his earnest best to do his duty, and it was a minor miracle.

The usual rule in any conflict is that the minor miracle should give right-of-way to the major, but Jerzy McBe's miracle did not extend to the recognition that was Sir Henry's due. McBe functioned—he didn't think.

He said, after clearing his throat, "Halt, there. Hold, Trog. I wish to see your papers." He raised his hand.

He wondered if it would make its throbbing noise again. He took absolutely no notice of a change in color from mostly-brown and white to the silks of an agrarian gentleman in gray and olive. Mere details. He had the principle of examining the papers of Trogs down by heart and he was as convinced as Sir Henry.

And soon he was more.

"I have no papers," said Sir Henry.

"Aha, then I have caught you. Let me formally take you into custody." McBe did not know the pertinent regulations, but he knew there were some for he had been told.

"But I don't need papers," Sir Henry said, regaining some of Sir Henry Oliphaunt. "I'm the new Empire Administrator here on Delbalso. Straighten up there, young man, and show me some respect."

"A Trog appointed Empire Administrator? I don't believe it. They wouldn't do that."

Sir Henry said, "I am not a Trog. I am Sir Henry Oliphaunt. I am wearing a costume for a masquerade. Do you like it?"

McBe said, "Well, no, sir. It makes me uncomfortable. Are you sure you aren't a Trog? You look like a Trog to me."

There were differences for the trained eye, but not to the eye of Jerzy McBe. It looked like a Trog to him. He kept ducking his head back from it in nervous impulse.

"No, I am the Empire Administrator." With emphasis, he said, "It can be quickly checked, Assistant."

"Yes, sir," said McBe. "But couldn't you take off your costume and show yourself to me?"

"No!" said Sir Henry the Trog. He was not ready to come out. Not yet. Not with the new angles, the new sharp perspectives, the patterns yet to see.

McBe began to insist, and the harder he insisted the harder Sir Henry resisted. And the more Sir Henry resisted, the more determined McBe was to insist.

It was a conflict in miracles, McBe given energy by his, and Sir Henry determined to defend his new view of the world at all cost. The narrower McBe's concentration, the better he functioned, and he narrowed his universe to the Trog. He brought out a restraint and began to maneuver to fasten it to the arm of the random Trog. Now that he had decided that it definitely must be the same old Trog up to his tricks, he was angry with it for having the nerve to suggest that it was anything so exalted as an Empire Administrator.

Sir Henry's major miracle was more fragile and could not stand exposure. He would not come out and he would not be restrained. So he backed away and wondered what noise he should make—whether he should growl, bark or roar.

"Give me your arm—that's a good Trog! Mind, now!"

Tentatively, Sir Henry said, *"Rrrf . . . Arf. Grr."* Then, loud and quite frightening: *"Rowr! Rowr!"* It was not what a genuine Trog would have said, particularly not an agrarian gentleman, but it took McBe aback.

He began to circle in again. Sir Henry padded back.

Sir Henry was saved by the advent of a troop of Xochitl Sodality members in the Red of Montague.

"Look," said one. "Just look."

And another said, "Take back the matched set of peels."

"But they grunt harmoniously."

"No matter. We have a new Wonder."

McBe sighed. He almost cried. And he was suddenly aware that his schedule was sadly awry and that he needed the use of a toilet again.

Sir Henry the Trog felt Wonderful. He felt truly Marvelous. Sir Henry the Trog.

"I am your Trog," he said.

9

HOLIDAYS ARE NO pleasure for anyone but children, and they are a pleasure for children only because they seem new. Holidays are no pleasure to those who schedule them. Holidays are for people who need to be formally reminded to have a good time and believe it is safer to warm up an old successful party than to chance the untried. And they sigh in relief when the ordeal is done.

And we sigh at the stale fare we are served in the name of pleasure. And the children sigh, too, the fifth or sixth time the holiday comes round.

Holidays purportedly give excuse for joy and celebration—but so does every day. Harvest, solstice, the birth of a baby. Any day offers excuse. Sir Henry Oliphaunt would tell you so. Sir Henry the Trog.

The best parties in the world are unscheduled, unheralded, unrehearsed events. And the best of the best, of course, are the sort co-opted by holidaymakers.

It is the fate of holidays when they grow old to be

131

celebrated only by historians. And the historians are kept busy because every day has been someone's holiday. Every day offers excuse for ecstasy. And the historians remain at their posts performing their ritual celebrations until they are called outside by song.

Lady Oliphaunt did not notice that the teeth of Ozu Xenakis were unattractively large, as Xenakis could not help but be aware. He wondered again whether he should have something done about them.

"It's no use your asking again," he said. "Your Mr. Villiers said he would be back in time to watch the Wonders and Marvels judging and that's all I know."

"But I've been *waiting*," she said. She came near to crying to demonstrate her distress, but decided not, on the ground that good effects should be used conservatively.

The *Centre* had more trade than earlier and Xenakis now had help. As Wonders and Marvels time approached, a few of the local curious with a taste for vulgar entertainment were beginning to stir. Those with money tended toward the *Centre*. And those without were beginning to think of finding places to watch underneath the peeltrees.

Xenakis did not mind speaking on someone else's subject—if business were not too pressing—but the subject of waiting was one he felt had had its hour. Lady Oliphaunt was paying for the use of his Private Rooms—in fact one room, not large, but with an excellent view of the green. This entitled her to his time and attention. Still he felt that men's subjects were more concrete and less emotional, and hence altogether more worthy.

"I'm sure he will be here soon, milady," he said. "I'll send him in directly as soon as he arrives."

He made to go, hoping she might not ring again. And if she did ring again, he hoped it might be to discuss a new topic. Something he could discover thoughts about. But she said hold.

"As long as I'm waiting," she said, "bring me a glass of hypon. And a dish of sugar-grass. Oh, and perhaps a few slices of ham. And maybe a piece of fruitcake. Do you have fruitcake?"

Xenakis said, "Yes, indeed. Would you like our domestic sugar-grass or sugar-grass imported from Moro?"

"Morovian sugar-grass," she said. "Of course."

"Yes, milady," he said. At the door he said, "The fruitcake is made with domestic fruit."

"That's all right," Lady Oliphaunt said.

Xenakis punched her order and picked up a waiting plate of blue cheese toasted on muffins. The plate was heaped with muffins. The white of the cheese had melted away leaving the blue tubular veins standing in a destructed landscape. Xenakis thought it looked hideous and deadly, but it was what the Orthodoxou in I.S. uniform had ordered.

Slyne was sufficiently upset to have set his sensory amplifier aside. He sat alone at a table equidistant from the windows and the door and the stimulations of the night. He was surprised and shocked by his collapse. It wasn't at all like him. At least, it had never happened before. He would have tolerated it in no one else, and tolerated it in himself only because he had to. But he did not enjoy the discovery of new weakness.

He found himself wondering about McBe and forced

his thoughts away. He turned away from the sensory amplifier. Even to see it was a strain on his overburdened senses.

He had come into the *Centre* to rest and calm his racing heart, but on the off-chance that part of his emotional state was due to hunger, he had ordered a simple favorite.

Without his sensory amplifier Slyne was revealed as harmonious if not overtly attractive. His head, as the rest of him, was covered with close black velvet. His eyes were surrounded by pink wrinkles. You might not think him pretty, but you could think him a pretty good Orthodoxou.

Slyne looked up only when his muffins-and-cheese were set before him. With his sensory amplifier in place he would have known much sooner. He ate every last muffin and found indeed they had a calming effect, but he still did not trust himself enough to don the amplifier. Instead he called Xenakis to the table.

"Have you seen any other Imperial Service personnel tonight?"

There! A solid subject. Something to talk and think about.

Xenakis said, "There were a couple of pantographers in here earlier tonight, but they got themselves taken on as Wonders and they're out playing."

"Pantographers? But I know them," said Slyne. "They're not Wonders."

"I thought not myself at first," said Xenakis. "They wanted to join, but they didn't seem like Wonders. I've seen a fair number of Marvels pass under my windows, you know. But, then, goodness, the way they showed how the stars influence us here on Delbalso was amazing. Did you know that Delbalso is a unique place?"

As is every planet. But Delbalso was unique in its own particular fashion, and Xenakis did honestly find that Marvelous.

"I wouldn't be at all surprised if they finished well," said Xenakis.

"Have you seen anyone in uniform?"

"No one but you."

"Oh. By any chance, have you seen a Trog?"

"I never have. Have you?"

"Oh, yes," said Slyne. "There is a Trog on Delbalso now and I have every intention of checking his papers."

"Well," said Xenakis, "I would suggest that you stay right here. The Xochitl Sodality will be gathering shortly on the green, and if there is a Trog on Delbalso, he's likely to be taken for a Marvel."

"Do you think so?" asked Slyne. But upon consideration he found that even he thought so. Possibly. "They gather soon?"

"Soon," said Xenakis.

"In that case, I'll have another plate of muffins," said Slyne. "And melt the cheese until the veins stick out."

The gathering of Xochitl Sodality was, in fact, to be soon. Xenakis had developed a fine sense for the rhythms of a Wonders and Marvels night in exactly the same manner as his uncanny knack for weather prediction based on the timbre of peelgrunt. It was a matter of experience.

Each House had its own preliminary gathering and selected its one best choice from the collected possibilities. Badrian Beaufils, as the man responsible for Joralemon House's Wonder, was named Official Locutor and he met with the Locutors from the other Houses. And it was only here and only at last that he was found by Ossian Chimmeroon.

"Ah, there, Friend Chimmeroon," said Badrian Beaufils. "Sit down on the bench. Have you come to watch the Wonders and Marvels judging?"

"I came out originally to bring you your friend Torve the Trog—and what a marvelous Wonder he would have made! But he was taken away out of hand by a bunch from Pierrepont. They draw no lines when it comes to winning."

"Oh, I've seen Torve," said Beaufils. "It's all right. We have a Marvel—now, let me tell you . . ."

But he was interrupted and called to join the conference of Official Locutors.

"Sit down," he said to Chimmeroon. "Sit down. I'll be back in a minute."

He left Ossian Chimmeroon sitting on his bench recovering his breath and his poise. And he was back in a minute.

"Ossian," he said, "as long as you aren't doing anything, would you run up to the *Centre* and find us some judges? And Ossian, pick some new faces. Let's not have Ozu Xenakis as a judge again."

"But he counts on it," said Chimmeroon. "It's the only reason he works on a Sodality night."

"Have you noticed that he favors Pierrepont Green?"

"All right," said Chimmeroon. "But only if I can give the Invocation."

Lady Oliphaunt had eaten her imported sugar-grass

and was half done with her domestic fruitcake when Villiers entered the *Centre*'s Private Rooms.

"At last!" she said. "Tony, where have you been?" There was a certain sharpness in her voice, token no doubt of five years of being Lady Oliphaunt. She had never been patient, but before her marriage she had not been given to sharpness.

"My apologies, Amita. I've had conflicting demands on my attention or I should certainly have been here sooner."

"But I've been *worried*," she said, taking a bite of fruitcake. Around the fruitcake she said, "I was beginning to think of all the terrible things that might have happened to you, and I was just frantic."

"Did Sir Henry accompany you to town, or is he yet at my uncle's?"

"Oh, let's not talk about Sir Henry," she said. "I've left him. He was *dancing in the streets* in that horrid costume and I turned the corner and he didn't even notice because I peeked back and he didn't even *notice* and I've left him. Tony, have some fruitcake?"

She said it hopefully and Villiers was polite enough not to reject offers of hospitality, at least those consonant with principle.

"Thank you," he said.

He stood as Lady Oliphaunt cut him a piece and when he reached for it she could not help but notice that the tip of his left little finger was missing. She exclaimed in surprise, waving the knife and threatening to separate larger pieces of anatomy.

"Oh!" she said. "Tony—you've hurt your finger." She then failed delicately, at least by indication.

"Yes," he said, "but not recently." He ate cake from his right hand and considered his left little finger as a unique object. It was more than Individuality and less than a Curiosity. It was an Object for Conversation.

"It happened in my last encounter with Livermore. The tip of my finger was exacted as a sacrifice to a beast-god in the name of wisdom."

It was the sort of thing that Lady Oliphaunt could easily imagine happening on Livermore, for, after all, she had been married there. On the other hand, while her life had been free, it had never been kinky, and there were some unnatural practices of which she was not sure she could honestly approve.

"Did you cooperate?" she asked.

"Oh, no," said Villiers. "It was all lightning happenstance."

He had been caught in a circle not of his own drawing and lost a little flesh, blood, fingernail and bone in clashing gears. But a nipped fingertip for wisdom is not a bad bargain. The established price is an eye.

"Oh," Lady Oliphaunt said with some relief. "That's fortunate. Tony, will you take me away from Delbalso?"

"If you mean will I escort you, of course I would be pleased," Villiers said. "It would be an honor, Lady Oliphaunt. But I feel I should warn you of a few things. Have you the money for your passage?"

"Well . . ." she said.

"As it happens," he said, "I do not."

"But," she said, "you're using a title now."

"Titles and money are independent variables. In fact, I seem to presume most upon my title when money is shortest."

"I do have some pin money," she said. "I suppose I can pay for passage."

"Ah, but the warning. A friend would travel with us."

Amita Oliphaunt set down the last of her fruitcake in a convult of suspicion.

"And who would your friend be?" she asked. "Do you have some *petite amie* with you?"

Inquiry after friends was a characteristic of hers that Villiers remembered well. One of her principal complaints about her husband was that he had so few active friends of any sort. It was incongruous, too, in that she herself liked to keep her family and friends well separate.

"Nothing like that," said Villiers. "This is the vegetarian friend I mentioned to you earlier."

It seemed to her that she did remember him making vague mention of a vegetarian friend and she was somewhat mollified. She could imagine no threat in a vegetarian, even a female.

But then Villiers added, "But this friend is a Trog."

"A Trog."

"Yes, a Trog. I hesitated to tell you earlier for fear of upsetting you unnecessarily, but if you are to travel with us, you really ought to know. His name is Torve."

"Do you mean this or are you joking? You really don't want to take me. Isn't that it?"

"Not at all," said Villiers. "It will be my personal delight to escort you. I simply thought that I had best warn you of your company."

She looked at him, as unable to decide as ever what

was going on in his mind. Villiers looked friendly, intelligent, composed and reserved and he was beyond her.

"I'll ask Harbourne Firnhaber to escort me," she said.

"If you like. I suspect, however, that it might cost you more than the price of your passage. Harbourne has neither money nor a title."

"Oh, yes," she said and paused to reconsider.

And it was while she was reconsidering that there was urgent approach in the hall and the door was thrown open. Lord Semichastny stood, framed in the doorway, but not filling it. Behind him was Ozu Xenakis with a plate of muffins covered with blue cheese, toasted.

Xenakis said, "In there."

Lady Oliphaunt said, "How . . ."

Villiers said, "Ah, Uncle . . ."

Uncle said, "Where is your husband?"

And he said, "Where is your costume, Lady Oliphaunt?"

And he said, "Where is *your* costume, Nephew? You were to have one picked out."

And he said, "I found another letter."

Joralemon House effectively ended Harbourne Firnhaber's hunt for Lord Semichastny's motley crowd. While he was waiting at Joralemon House the suspicion that Lord Semichastny's recommendation, valuable as it might be, was not worth his present eternal achronic state of wretchedness, blitzed briefly in his mind leaving behind a glowing question. After Joralemon House, his steps slowed and he began to engage in earnest converse with himself. After Joralemon House, he began to think of quitting.

He stopped knocking on doors. He shouted on no streetcorners. And he decided at last not even to raise the subject of parties unless someone were to ask.

From perfunctory, his efforts became nominal. He simply walked the streets thinking vaguely of what he was supposed to be doing and feeling inadequate to do it. Then from nominal his effort became nonexistent.

He sat down on a public seat by the side of the road and said, flatly and definitely, "I quit." And he found relief in the admission. His anxiety departed and he began to try to set his excuses in order:

He had tried.

He hadn't been able to find anyone. He hadn't known where to look.

He had looked, but it was dark.

Nobody had wanted to come. He had asked, but *every single person* he had met had turned him down.

It wasn't his fault.

And after a time he had his case in hand and his anecdotes trimmed to fit. Only then did he check the time, and to his horror he saw that he had dawdled too long. It was fully, fully time for Lord Semichastny's party.

He thought of his alternatives, and decided at last to have a drink.

It was some time before Jules and Miriam Parini set out for Lord Semichastny's country maison. Their best cherry-picking clothes had been packed for travel, and they would not have even considered going to Lord Semichastny's party in anything else.

Parini's cherry-picking suit was his most stylish, the only suit he owned that could allow him to pass as something more than a rug salesman with social ambitions. It was the suit in which he had encountered the scrutiny of the interviewing alumna from Miss McBurney's and passed inspection. He rated that as a heart-held triumph second only to the amount of tuition Miss McBurney allowed him to pay.

And not only were the clothes stylish, but they had a sufficiency of pockets, a detail modern tailors are prone to overlook.

Dressing Annie suitably in tight black took some time, too. There were on occasion little things for a little girl to do and Parini felt that it was not an auspicious time to find someone to watch her, so he dressed her in black and took her along.

Before they left, the mail from Duden came.

Annie reproved the mailman by saying, *"Beng,"* in severe tones.

"There," said Mrs. Parini. But Parini thought that reproof was deserved and so he did not speak to his daughter.

Villiers took the letter that his uncle held. It had been opened, no doubt by oversight. It is extremely easy to open an envelope without checking the formal address. He looked at the letter only long enough to see that it was from Louisa Parini at Miss McBurney's Justly Famous Seminary and Finishing School on Nashua, and put it away unread.

"Thank you," said Villiers. "I believe that Sir Henry is still in his Trog costume and if I make no mistake, I think you can see him in a few minutes being judged as a Marvel on the green below."

He waved to the windows.

"Well, you've certainly failed me, then, haven't you?" asked Lord Semichastny. "Was this our understanding? Give me the letter back."

Villiers said, "I believe you confuse me with Harbourne Firnhaber, sir. We have no agreements."

"Oh, yes. Harbourne! Charteris, you are not serving my interests as you ought. If you expect me to locate this missing money of yours, you'll go find Sir Henry and bring him back to the house for the party."

Lady Oliphaunt laughed shortly. "Are you going to invite me to the party as well?"

"But of course you're coming. I'll have Charles find you a costume. You could try Semiramis Among the Doves."

"It wouldn't suit me," she said.

Villiers said, "However, Uncle, I do have a suggestion. A considerable number of people are shortly to meet on the green, including Sir Henry. Bring your party here."

"Bring what? Bring the party . . . I don't like it. Let the people come to me."

"An excellent policy," said Villiers. "The question is whether they will come."

Lord Semichastny began to pace and growl. He said, "No," under his breath and he slammed a toe into the wall. He swung around and looked angrily at Villiers. He was more successful in intimidating Lady Oliphaunt, who had developed a certain shyness of him.

He said, "But it isn't right. They're *Monists*."

Villiers said, "I've heard both you and them spoken well of in all but the same breath."

"By whom?"

"By our host, Mr. Xenakis."

"He doesn't know me very well," Lord Semichastny said. "Did he really?"

"Yes, indeed."

"What did he say about me?"

At that point, Villiers knew he had the argument won. The argument was clinched when there was a light rap on the door. Villiers opened to Xenakis.

"Ah," Villiers said, but Lord Semichastny did not take advantage of this opportunity to ask Xenakis his opinion directly, though Xenakis would have given it. Lord Semichastny had his opportunity for direct communication and let it pass by. No wonder he was considered difficult.

Xenakis said, "Mr. Chimmeroon from the Xochitl Sodality is here. He wants some judges for the Wonders and Marvels contest." Xenakis was greatly disappointed not to be wanted as a judge himself, but was carrying on well.

"How many does he need?" Lord Semichastny asked.

"Three," said Xenakis. "Was I right to ask?"

At the door of the house, Jerzy McBe nodded his thanks to the nice lady. He had knocked seeking relief, and found not only relief but refreshment. She had offered him jellyroll, but he had turned it down in favor of cookies and sympathy. He had not expected hospitality and understanding, and ordinarily would not have been aware of them, but on this particular night he was receptive to an offer of cookies and sympathy. He didn't care much for jellyroll.

"Thank you, ma'am," he said. "This has been a

welcome hour. If you are ever up at the Castle, come
through my line.''

"Can't you stay?" she said.

"No, ma'am," he said. "I've got a job to do."

The power of cookies and sympathy as a restorative
has too long been underestimated. McBe set out again
in Trog pursuit.

The Xochitl Sodality in ones and twos and threes, in
blue and green and red and yellow, strolled in a passing
parade down the street and then down the stairway to
the park and the green. Harbourne Firnhaber stood on
the steps leading up to the *Centre* and watched the
middle-aged men pass.

Harbourne had the impulse to call down and ask
them if they wanted to go to a party, but he didn't.
Instead, he resented them for appearing now that his
mind had been made up. He had his excuses in very
good order, such as they were. But then he wondered if
these strange men might not be fitted into his story. The
Xochitl Sodality. But as villains or as humor?

He turned and took the stairs, feeling very much in
need of his drink. He reached for the door only to have
it open in front of him.

It was Lord Semichastny. Behind him were Lord
Charteris and Lady Oliphaunt.

The encounter was completely unexpected by Harbourne Firnhaber. His heart beat wildly and he was
swept with a wave of cold. He felt discovered.

"There you are, Nephew," said Lord Semichastny.
"Be a good boy, Harbourne, and run out to the house
and bring my party to the green. I'll have Charles and
all the serving mechanicals. And make a point of bringing some melons."

10

NOTHING IS IMMORTAL, not even the universe. Nothing is immortal but change. And change means mortality. Mortality is the one central fact with which every self-aware being must deal. It is every man for himself in the wrestle with death.

The most presumptuous thing to ask of any mortal being is to wait. There are none so visibly involved with death as those condemned to wait.

Those who wait squander their little time, and they know it. They wait for change, change of any sort, for change is hope of life.

Charles the Butler told of the fate of the old man. He was eaten. He told of the fate of the old woman. She was eaten. He told of what happened to the little household robot. She was carried off, but eventually she was rescued.

And poor little dog Turpie.

The thrust of justice and fate in the story was so overwhelming that the gathered mechanicals were struck dumb with pity and terror. In the hush that followed the story, the growing sound of a flitter could be heard. The mechanicals shivered and their gears clenched.

"Be calm," said Charles. "Be calm. It's time for the party."

He straightened his tarboosh and bade them all stay. He rolled to the front door and waited there beside the glass urn filled with flower petals, purple, white, yellow and pink. At last the door opened and Harbourne Firnhaber entered. Charles dipped out double handfuls of flower petals and strewed them in the air.

"Welcome," he said. "Welcome."

While Harbourne Firnhaber was down in Lord Semichastny's cold cellar picking out a variety of his best melons, Charles gave instructions to the serving table that was to be left in charge when all the other mobile mechanicals had gone.

"But I'd like to go, too," the serving table said.

"Someone has to stay. Someone has to be in charge."

"I was counting on serving tonight. This is my most attractive set of attachments."

"I know," said Charles.

But when Harbourne Firnhaber and Charles and all the other mobile mechanicals, and all the food, music and celebration had been loaded, and all had departed the house, the serving table was left behind. It rolled disconsolately from room to room, feeling the size of its responsibility.

"Food," it said plaintively. "Drink. Stimulants of all sorts. Canapé? Amygdala? Maybe a salt olive?"

It raised its serving covers half-heartedly. But no one answered. The house was empty.

The serving table swept back and forth through the house. Responsible. Alone. And it sang:

" 'The joys of future years are past, tomorrow's hopes have fled away. Still, let us love, and e'en at last we shall be happy yesterday.' "

But music provided no consolation. And then at last there was the sound of another flitter outside.

The serving table rolled to the door and waited. It did not dip double handfuls of flower petals because it lacked the capability with this set of attachments. And it waited for what seemed the longest time before the door sounded. The table tripped the door release.

Standing on the step were a middle-aged couple in formal dress and with them was a young female child dressed all in black.

"We were invited to a party here," said the man.

The table said, "The party has been moved to town. It's to take place on the public green as part of some Monist celebration."

"Oh," said the man. But he made no move to go. Indeed, after a brief moment he waved the little girl and the woman forward.

"I'm sorry, sir," said the table, "but I can't allow you inside. No, really, sir."

"We'll only have a brief look around and be gone before you know it," the man said inexorably.

The table protested. "My instructions are firm. You aren't supposed to be within the house. I'm afraid I'll have to put you out by force."

It realized that it lacked the right attachments, but it was determined. It circled them and tried to herd them back toward the open door. It nudged the little girl.

"Go on," it said. "Go on."

The little girl stepped back abruptly and reached for her mother's skirts. "Mommy!"

Her mother said, "Get away from her, you table."

The man, hardly seeming to notice, shined his light around the entry hall of the maison. The woman shooed the table back. It circled, looking for advantage, and then rolled forward again.

The little girl dipped into the urn of flower petals and threw a handful at the table. *"Hobyah! Hobyah!"* she said.

The table fled, and who could wonder.

The woman said, "Do you see, Jules? Aren't you ever going to say anything to her?"

11

THE VERY BEST parties in all the world are unscheduled, unheralded and unrehearsed.

The three judges sat in the middle of the green on a small one-step platform with Ossian Chimmeroon and the four Locutors. On each of the four sides of the green stood the four Houses in their colors, surrounding their Marvels like secrets.

Anthony Villiers sat at ease waiting for the judging to begin. He opened the letter that Lord Semichastny had handed him and read it for the first time, a quick scan, and then he put it away.

Lord Semichastny, having made his decision, was determined to enjoy himself. He took quick little glances around. He talked to Lady Oliphaunt and took a sweet little pinch on her cheek. She took the opportunity shortly thereafter to switch her seat, but he did not notice because he was asking a question of Rafael Abdelnoor, the Locutor of Schermerhorn House.

Lady Oliphaunt was somewhat less quick to adjust to her role of judge. She wasn't sure she cared to judge Trogs.

She looked around restlessly. She could see faces at the windows of the *Centre* and other people here and there among the trees under the swaying somnolent peels.

She said to Ossian Chimmeroon, "Don't you *mind* being watched?"

"Oh, no, ma'am," said Ossian Chimmeroon. "It's one of the best ways we have for recruiting Monists."

Lady Oliphaunt noticed Villiers' quick look at the letter from Louisa Parini.

"And who was that from?" she asked.

"Another friend," he said.

"Another Trog?"

"No," he said. "A girl."

She turned from him to Ossian Chimmeroon. She said in a careless voice, "Tell me, Mr. Chimmeroon. What do you think of our Princess-Gillian-to-be?"

It was a question for Ozu Xenakis, meaty and with lots of room for honest unconsidered opinion. As it happened, however, while Ossian Chimmeroon was not good at spur-of-the-moment opinion, this was a question to which he had given thought. The Emperor's new daughter-in-law was a topic of interest even in Monist Houses.

"She doesn't have much of a figure," he said. "And her posture is bad. She slumps her shoulders and slouches her hips. But the report I have is that her voice is excellent."

"It would have to be," said Lady Oliphaunt.

"Excuse me, now," said Ossian Chimmeroon. "It's time for the Invocation."

He stood and spread his arms. He called for silence and waved the Sodality closer, and they moved around him, their Marvels well-sequestered. It was the moment.

Invocation was the prerogative of a man of dignity like Ossian Chimmeroon, and he made the most of the opportunity. His voice rolled sonorously over the gathered heads. He used dignified fat phrases such as "judgment among the stars" and "this time-hallowed tradition" and "the pure simplicity of our way of life." No one now could have said that he lacked manner.

He introduced the judges and they stood to their own round of applause. Lord Semichastny waved his hands over his head in acknowledgment. Lady Oliphaunt smiled politely, and nodded. Villiers smiled, too, and stood waiting quietly until the applause slackened, and then sat down.

The Houses had drawn lots for order of presentation, and Schermerhorn was first.

Chimmeroon motioned to Rafael Abdelnoor. "Go ahead, Friend Rafe," he said. "Bring out Schermerhorn's Marvel."

Abdelnoor swept off his bonnet in signal to the men of Schermerhorn, and was given a few hoots for the gesture from the other Houses. Schermerhorn split open and there was their double marvel. The astrologers stepped forward. There was only light applause because their skills were subtle, not obvious.

Sotto voce, Lady Oliphaunt asked Villiers, "Where is Sir Henry?" She had spotted a Trog surrounded by green and thought it must be her husband, but she was not sure.

However, Villiers pointed behind them into the mass

of the Red of Montague. She looked where he pointed and saw Sir Henry the Trog waiting his turn to be called as a Marvel, and it was only then that she completely believed Villiers. As much as she completely believed anyone.

Rafael Abdelnoor gave his astrologers a substantial build-up, and then they took over for themselves. They explained—in simple non-technical language suitable for middle-aged Sodality members—their computations and calculations for the Universal Pantograph Project. They told how they determined the influences of the stars. They added their private opinions—for, after all, they were pantographers only by profession. By avocation they were astrologers, and it meant that they had some special ideas of their own.

Like all pantographers. Like all astrologers.

All in all, they managed to show themselves as very clever fellows and to convince the onlookers that Delbalso was a most special and favored place out of all the places in the universe. At their conclusion they received applause that was distinctly enthusiastic.

"I really will hate to leave this planet after all these years," Lord Semichastny remarked.

"It's a Wonderful place," said Ossian Chimmeroon. The astrologers were good enough to sway even him for the moment, because he agreed so heartily with their conclusions, but then it was the turn of Joralemon House and his sympathies quickly became properly reestablished.

"Joralemon House," he said. "Badrian, here's your opportunity."

Badrian Beaufils gave a whoop and a holler and led Joralemon House in leading the Sodality and spectators in applause for Mr. Dodd, the Christian Historian. The applause was louder from the Sodality than the spectators, louder from Joralemon House than from the Sodality, and loudest of all from Badrian Beaufils.

"This one doesn't look like much to me," said Lord Semichastny, beginning to take an interest in his work. He sat up and waited skeptically for Dodd to prove himself Marvelous.

Lady Oliphaunt took advantage of the moments of Dodd's approach in study of Tony Villiers' friend the Trog. Brown, basically. He made her exceedingly nervous. He seemed to be staring back at her with great bulgy blue eyes. She looked away.

Dodd took the step up to the platform. He acknowledged the applause and thanked the crowd. Then he was properly introduced by Badrian Beaufils, and he did his level best to look modest.

"A Christian," said Lady Oliphaunt, who disapproved of kinkiness.

"True, true," said Zimmerman, the Locutor from Pierrepont, disparaging what he could not have. Everyone knows that the Christian beyond reach is sour.

But even Lord Semichastny had to admit that Dodd's tonsure chart was truly Marvelous. And by the time Dodd had finished with the story of Epiphany and Twelfth Night, both chock-full of historical anecdote, Zimmerman was quivering with the suppressed urge to carol and Lady Oliphaunt was at least listening.

In the interstice between Marvels, Lord Semichastny said, "This is excellent good fun, Charteris. In my spare moments I'm trying to think where your money might have been misplaced. That is, of course, if it ever came."

"To be sure," said Villiers.

After the showing of his Marvel, Badrian Beaufils looked very pleased with himself. "All right, Montague. Have your turn," he said.

Lady Oliphaunt turned to look at her husband. Sir Henry's turn.

"And now we shall judge Trogs," said Lady Oliphaunt.

"Oh, yes," said Villiers. "The best saved until last."

She said, "But Tony, how can you travel with a Trog? How can you ever trust it not to turn on you?"

"He trusts me not to turn on him, and thus far we have both been fortunate. I used to be on similar terms with my stomach until we agreed to disagree."

The discussion was ended by the anticipatory cheers for Sir Henry the Trog. The men of Montague opened a way for him to the platform, and there were ohs and ahs as well as cheers and applause. Sir Henry nodded and pranced toward the platform. He was self-evident. Introduction was not needed.

Montague's Locutor smiled. Montague doubled the applause that Joralemon had mustered.

The only restraint was from Pierrepont Green. As Sir Henry jogged, shook his trotters, popped his eyes of pseudo-Trog-Blue, hopped and cavorted, they saw their own Trog Marvel—apparently one of a more phlegmatic temperament—fade into a paler copy. Some of them looked at Torve in near-accusation. The only satisfaction for Pierrepont was in foretasting the chagrin of the Reds of Montague. Even a dancing Trog is small change if everyone has one.

And all three judges had reservations. Even if the Sodality members of Pierrepont were unpracticed enough to see a rare, unique and genuine Trog as a mere copy-Trog, and a copy-Trog as genuine, Villiers was one who knew the difference. Lord Semichastny only knew and believed in copy-Trogs. He had been one himself, so he necessarily held the crowd too easily swayed. Lady Oliphaunt's reservations have already been presented.

But still—for a copy-Trog, Sir Henry was very persuasive. He had put his hours of night practice to good use in the service of felicity, facility and fidelity. If he did not move to the platform with the certifiable pad of a true Trog, he did move with confidence and grace, and more important, he believed in himself. As the only Trog he knew, he could be the beau ideal of the Trog, and he fulfilled that beau ideal so well that he was sure he was a Trog.

Shakespeare, lacking a dictionary, was free. Believe it. Sir Henry, lacking any more guide than a few scraps of second-hand information, had been free to mold his characterization as his sense of art directed, and he had created "Sir Henry the Trog" from the well of his secret heart. There had never been an appropriate moment in Sir Henry's life for him to express charm and sweetness and lose himself in dance. It would have been inconsistent with the Sir Henry that had always been.

But he took charm and sweetness and the pounding freedom of dance and poured them into his Troggish creation. He could not have said why, except that it did seem appropriate.

He had only hoped in wearing this Trog costume that his friendliness and good intentions might be apparent to the world, and to his intoxication they were—except to those very few with cherished and deep-seated prejudice against Trogs. A number which must be a small minority.

To a purist, he was not a Trog. But be not overly taken with exact categorizations. He deserved his applause: his style of Trog was quite Wonderful.

Feeling the full swell of his agrarian soul, this gentleman farmer did a Paddy Dance of his own spontaneous creation. Lord Semichastny had once had some notion of Sir Henry Oliphaunt in costume all alone waltzing. Now to Sir Henry the Trog, the platform, the judges, his wife, and the Sodality in their colors making a flower around them all paled. In his mind he was standing up to his knees in a paddy, surrounded by others of his kind splashing and stomping out their joy of life.

Oh, the wildness! His eyes were closed. He was oblivious to the whistles and cheers, the fascinated faces. He stomped and squelched in muddy abandon.

And then there was a parting in the ranks of the Green of Pierrepont, and Torve the Trog stepped forward into the open. It was not his turn yet. Sir Henry's presentation on behalf of Montague House was not complete. Of those who saw Torve, some were astonished, some were curious, and some thought it a hideous breach of manners. It was *not* his turn.

Torve hopped up to the platform beside Sir Henry. Two Trogs, one brown-and-white (with a few black stripes, very faint), the other gray-and-olive. Of much the same size, a fair match, a fair pair. One with eyes of truer blue.

Sir Henry did not notice Torve's approach. He was lost, his eyes yet closed.

Torve stepped in front of Sir Henry, put four-fingered furry hands on his shoulders and squared him away. Sir Henry opened his eyes and saw what he had seen with his eyes closed—another Trog. Sir Henry put his four-fingered furry hands on Torve's shoulders.

"Dance!" he said. "Dance!"

And Torve did dance. Together they frolicked their way through the Paddy Dance. As could be plainly seen from his coat, Torve had no experience of paddies, but he recognized a Paddy Dance when he saw one. There wasn't a spectator watching to whom the dance did not communicate paddies.

They danced warmly, freely, meeting, separating, stomping and bogging. It was warm, exciting, captivating to watch. The dance went on, finding its proper shape, and even those who at first had blamed Torve, then reluctantly pardoned him as an ignorant alien, now found themselves approving of him wholeheartedly.

At last the dance ended and applause exploded in imminent conjugation. Sir Henry and Torve bathed in the warmth, and Torve relaxed to the oncoming swell of event.

When the applause had begun to fade and the moment was ripe, Torve turned again to Sir Henry. As he had done before, he put his hands on Sir Henry's shoulders and squared him away. When Sir Henry was squared, Torve drew back his furry spatulate foot and kicked Sir Henry in the leg with full deliberate power.

The crowd went, "Oooh."

Sir Henry cried and fell to the platform. Torve stood above him looking down, said, *"Thurb,"* very positively, and then turned and walked back to the Green of Pierrepont.

Lady Oliphaunt stood and said, "There! What did I tell you," speaking to Sir Henry, to Villiers, or to herself. She sighed, and then she sighed again, a sigh broken off in exasperation. She took one step toward Sir Henry, and then another.

"Darling!" she said. "Oh, what have you done to yourself? Oh, what have you done?"

Sir Henry said nothing in return, but lay looking after Torve, coming to realizations. And nursing his leg. He now had more data about Trogs.

Lady Oliphaunt fell to her knees and gathered him up and only then did he look at her with real recognition.

"Amita," he said. "What are you doing here?"

Jerzy McBe pushed his way through the crowd surrounding the Xochitl Sodality, surrounding the platform. The people were applauding the two Trogs. As he burst into the open, one Trog kicked the other and walked away.

He was faced with a choice and after a moment of indecision, he chose the immobile one. Of course.

"There you are, Trog," he said, looking down at Sir Henry Oliphaunt. "I want a look at your papers."

"He's not a Trog," said Lady Oliphaunt. "He's my husband."

"I'm not a Trog. I'm the Empire Administrator, Sir Henry Oliphaunt."

"I'm here, McBe. I'm here," came a voice behind McBe, and McBe turned with great relief. It was Slyne.

But it was Slyne with a difference. It was Slyne with his sensory amplifier in his hands and hideous pink wrinkles around his eyes.

Even without his sensory amplifier, Slyne could

smell. He smelled the delicious flavor of Jerzy McBe. He whuffled.

"What is going on?" asked Slyne. He was torpid with blue cheese and muffins and had lost track.

"Sir, I have your Trog," said Jerzy McBe.

"He does not," said Lady Oliphaunt.

Slyne looked at Sir Henry, and lacking the benefit of his sensory amplifier, which would surely have told him the difference, he said, "Oh, yes. Very good, McBe. Sir, Trog, if you please, I would examine your papers."

Jerzy McBe looked at Slyne with unrequited horror. He said, "Please, sir. Could you put your amplifier back on?"

Lady Oliphaunt said, "Show them, Henry. Please."

He nodded and she helped him to his feet. And then, to the amazement of almost all, he began to emerge from his Troggish self like a butterfly shucking a cocoon, wet and shining and newborn.

Slyne did not need his amplifier to tell that this was no Trog. He donned it hurriedly to find what he was facing—in the process bringing McBe great relief. And he found that he recognized what he was facing.

"Sir Henry Oliphaunt," he said. "Sir."

But Sir Henry was staring around him at the wide, wide world and discovering to his joy and exaltation that he still wanted to dance.

The sound of a flight of flitters could be heard in the dark night and the sound came closer and closer and then the flitters were setting down on the green itself. Robots popped out and began setting up tables and spreading out food.

As they began to play music, Lord Semichastny stood and said, "The food and music await you."

The assembly cheered, because it had been a long night. They turned and began to move toward the waiting repast.

Lord Semichastny tapped Villiers on the shoulder. "Here, Nephew. I just discovered this. It must have been left in the pocket the last time I wore this coat."

It was a money order for fifteen royals.

12

LORD SEMICHASTNY'S ENTERTAINMENT was held to be a
great success and hugely enjoyed by the Xochitl Sodality and such unaffiliated onlookers as cared to join.
They fed, wandered, wondered, talked and mingled.
They speculated as to which was more Marvelous, a
Trog, or a Trog that was more than just a Trog. They
listened to the music and to a story told by Charles to a
collected circle. They talked to the various Marvels and
before the night was done the astrologers were casting
individual horoscopes and Mr. Dodd, the Christian
Historian, had admitted that sometimes he thought he
was not just a historian, sometimes he thought he believed.

Ossian Chimmeroon approached Lord Semichastny
as he was signing Harbourne Firnhaber's self-
composed recommendation. (Who, after all, knew his
virtues so well?)

"Congratulation, Friend Semichastny," said Chimmeroon. "This is a delightful party. It's a pity that we all did not know each other sooner. I most particularly enjoyed that luscious orange-red melon."

"Did you like that?" asked Lord Semichastny. "That's one of my own favorites, sir. It's an Olatunge."

They talked melons briefly, and then Chimmeroon burst out, "It's really not right that your neighbors should force you out with this Winter-Summer Law. You have more friends than you know."

"Do I?" asked Lord Semichastny. "Who?"

"We, the Monists of Delbalso. We are not inconsiderable friends to have. We'll see about that law."

And he nodded emphatically.

Lord Semichastny looked after Chimmeroon as he walked away. Then he handed Harbourne his recommendation.

"Monists," he said. "I don't understand them."

Harbourne reached into his coat and found the brochures he had been given at Joralemon House.

"Here you are, sir," he said.

Before long Parini arrived and did a little cherry-picking before he came across Villiers. Villiers introduced him to Torve.

"Is pleasure," said Torve. "I have met your daughter Louisa."

"So I understand," Parini said, not looking at him directly. And then he said, "Your papers arrived." But he handed them to Villiers.

Villiers handed them to Torve. "Thank you, sir," he said. "How did your evening go?"

"Profitably. And yours, Mr. Villiers?"

"Moderately profitably. Shall we settle on a price for the name?"

They dickered and concluded at a mutually satisfactory eight royals. However, Parini was unable to give Villiers change for his money order, so Villiers sent Torve to find Lord Semichastny.

Lord Semichastny came within minutes, putting his Joralemon House brochures away. "These are fascinating people, Charteris," he said. "I've even been talking to some of them."

Villiers introduced him to Parini.

"I'm sure I've encountered the name before," said Lord Semichastny, and indeed he had.

Parini said, "Oh, I doubt it very much, sir. We are not a prominent family."

Lord Semichastny proved to be able to change the money order and was willing to do it for only two percent. He took his two percent and went off to talk to more Monists. Villiers took his share, and handed the rest to Parini.

"The name?" he said.

Parini said, "The man who hired Solomon 'Biff' Dreznik to kill you was your brother, Robinet Villiers."

Villiers nodded. "Thank you," he said.

"Excuse me, Sir Trog," Slyne said through his sensory amplifier. McBe hung at his heels. "May I see your Red Card and your Permit to Travel? Apparently through oversight they were not inspected when you arrived at the Castle."

"Certainly," said Torve, and handed them to the Orthodoxou.

On their way to Castle Rock, Mrs. Parini said, "I've been wondering, Jules."

"About what?"

"What do you think of the possibility of Villiers and Louisa?"

"Villiers and Louisa what?"

"Becoming interested in each other."

"What?" he said. "I should see my daughter tied to such a humorless man? Oh, no, I have plans for Louisa. I want her to learn to *act* like a lady, not become one."

Anthony Villiers and Torve the Trog left the party before dawn, before the party was fully done. They went to Castle Rock and took passage from Delbalso.

Torve said goodbye separately to Badrian Beaufils, and Villiers spoke to Sir Henry and Lady Oliphaunt.

Lady Oliphaunt said, "Be careful of your friend, Tony."

Villiers said, "We must judge by result, not by what we see."

"I am," she said soberly.

On their way to the port, Villiers said, "By the way, I had a letter from Louisa Parini. She says that Alice Tutuila and Norman Adams are to be married soon on Nashua, and we are invited. That makes two weddings we are called to attend on Nashua. I don't see how we can refuse."

"No. Is all right," said Torve the Trog. "Soon,

165

though, I think I wish to journey homewards to Trogholm.''

''We'll do that,'' said Villiers.

They left Delbalso in second-class accommodations on a good ship. They left Delbalso as the sun was turning Castle Rock from black to slanting marble.

In spite of her doubts, Lady Oliphaunt found Sir Henry and herself growing reconciled. The beginning of her stay on Delbalso was moderately tedious because of the Winter-Summer Laws, but after less than two years they were repealed and life then livened considerably so that when the end of Sir Henry's largely successful administration was done, she actually regretted leaving Delbalso to return to Sir Henry's country estates on Trefflewood.

Lord Semichastny did not leave Delbalso. He stayed, even under the strictures of the Winter-Summer Laws. In fact, after two months of consideration, he joined the Delbalso Monist Association and went to live at Joralemon House. He donated his country maison to the Monist Association and it became Coppersmith House, though there were scattered votes for ''Semichastny House.'' Charles the Robot managed the place very successfully for the Monists, as he had for Lord Semichastny. He joined the Monist Association himself, and was held in high regard by his fellows. His Monist career was so successful that he was able to convince two friends in the Merry Major-Domos to join. And he was never ever required to wear orange—unless you should consider the Copper of Coppersmith House to be a shade of orange.

In spite of his glowing recommendation from Lord

Semichastny, Harbourne Firnhaber did not feel ready to tackle Nashua. So he sat on random shelves for several more years and continued to ripen.

Sir Henry Oliphaunt kept his Trog suit. He never wore it and he never spoke of it to Lady Oliphaunt, but he kept the suit and sometimes late at night he would take it from its secret place and look at it. And there were other nights when he would suddenly rise from his chair and dance around the room.

In THE UNIVERSAL PANTOGRAPH, the fourth Anthony Villiers adventure, such universals are discussed as Nominalism, Realism, marriage, the Great Ian Steele Contest, and Louisa Parini. To follow soon.

A
Science
Fiction
Western
and
Motorcycle
Quest
Epic!

$1.95

PRO

An illustrated novel of interplanetary adventure!

$1⁹⁵

An Ace illustrated novel of gripping inter-planetary adventure from Gordon R. Dickson, multiple Hugo and Nebula winning author of DORSAI! and TIME STORM—a pro in his own right.

Over 50 pages of illustrations by the author's favorite artist—James Odbert.

ACE SCIENCE FICTION **360 PARK AVENUE SOUTH • NEW YORK, N.Y. 100**

PROJECT PROMETHEUS WOULD STEAL THE FIRE OF THE SUN—
BUT THE PRICE MIGHT BE TOO TERRIBLE TO CONTEMPLATE.

A NOVEL OF THE NEAR FUTURE BY
HARRY HARRISON
SKYFALL

ACE
SCIENCE
FICTION

$1.95

360 PARK AVENUE SOUTH • NEW YORK, N.Y. 10010